"*The (Diblos) Note[...]* [...] icture of the Hesitation W[...] [...]n angel, the writer, for its [...] [...]ny book that deals so honestly with the sin of consciousness, and its island setting is a little paradise lost. I read it with pangs of recognition."

—**Mary McCarthy**

"This is the kind of novel it is a pleasure to take seriously, a disciplined, adventurous performance in the best tradition of fictional experiment."

—**Wilfrid Sheed,** *New York Times Book Review*

"*The (Diblos) Notebook* is a genuine and unpretentious work of art. . . . Its true subject is its own manner and style, its elusive, almost furtive brilliance, so that the book really is about the poetic impression, the quick insight, the misunderstanding, the discarded sketch as opposed to the constructed and finished museum piece."

—**John Thompson,** *New York Review of Books*

"Sparkles with poetic dialogue and description and is full of a wry humor which is alternately sophisticated and mocking in the best mock-heroic satiric tradition. . . . This is a fine, important, and eminently readable novel, highly recommended."

—*Library Journal*

# BOOKS BY JAMES MERRILL

*Poetry*

Selected Poems 1946-1985
The Inner Room
Late Settings
From the First Nine: Poems 1946-1976
The Changing Light at Sandover
Divine Comedies
Braving the Elements
The Fire Screen
Nights and Days
Water Street
The Country of a Thousand Years of Peace
First Poems

*Novels*

The (Diblos) Notebook
The Seraglio

*Plays*

The Bait
The Immortal Husband

*Essays*

Recitative

*Memoirs*

A Different Person

# JAMES MERRILL

# THE
# (DIBLOS)
# NOTEBOOK

DALKEY ARCHIVE PRESS

First published in 1965 by Atheneum Publishers
© 1965 by James Merrill
Afterword © 1994 by James Merrill

First Dalkey Archive Edition, 1994

Library of Congress Cataloging-in-Publication Data
Merrill, James Ingram.
   The (Diblos) notebook / James Merrill ; with an afterword
by the author. — 1st Dalkey Archive ed.
   1. Novelists, American—Greece—Fiction. 2. Fiction
—Authorship—Fiction. 3. Americans—Greece—Fiction.
I. Title.
PS3525.E6645D45   1994   813'.54—dc20   94-9180
ISBN 1-56478-064-3

Partially funded by grants from the National Endowment for
the Arts and the Illinois Arts Council.

NATIONAL
ENDOWMENT
FOR ❤ THE
A R T S

Dalkey Archive Press
Illinois State University
Campus Box 4241
Normal, IL 61790-4241

*Printed on permanent/durable acid-free paper and bound in the
United States of America*

*Isidore a menti, je ne méprise personne*
*et ne hais point mes parents.*

Ayoub Sinano, *Artagal*

~~Orestes~~

The islands of Greece

Across vivid water the islands of Greece lie. They have been cut out of cardboard and set on bases of

at subtle odds with one another, upon bases of pale haze. Their colors are mauve, exhausted blue, tanned rose, here & there crinkled to catch the light. They do not seem

It is inconceivable that they are of one substance with the warm red rock underfoot

rock of one's own vantage point ( ? )

One early evening

(Name) had grown used to this contradiction. She

Late one ~~spring~~ afternoon a woman no longer ~~puz~~ ~~zled~~ troubled by this illusion left her house, the largest on the island of (Name), and set out on foot in the direction of town.

At the top of a hill she met Orestes. He

Her body was strong and graceful, her features first darkened, then silvered by the dry summer. White strands in her iron-colored hair shot backward into an elaborate plaited bun. Her ~~large, Byzantine~~ eyes, immense & shining, though set in webs of age, attended without curiosity to the path which rose and fell never far from the water's edge. She wore sandals, a gray skirt, not embroidered, & a night-blue shawl

and had wound a thin night-blue shawl around the upper part of her body, to produce an impression of deliberate, coquettish antiquity. Drawstring looped over her wrist, an old-fashioned beaded purse sparkled mustily as she walked, making light of the mission she did not have. She had told them she was going to the pharmacy. They had

She had said she was going to the pharmacy, not that there was anything to do, now, but wait. The others had appeared to understand.

So did the few people she passed; they greeted her courteously, without lingering.

On a small promontory she met Orestes. He was walking away from the town. It stretched on either side of him like a robe, its hues of white & stone hanging down into the still harbor.

"Pardon me," he said. "Do you live here? I am looking for the Sleeping Woman."

His Greek, fluent but incorrect, made her examine him carefully.

"Ah," she said at length, "but the best view is from the town. Did no one point it out? You must turn back."

Whereupon they fell into step together and Orestes set about

O., who found all his own traits extraordinary, set about marveling at his ~~stupidity~~ imperception. Did she mean those slopes directly facing the port? *Their* silhouette made up the Sleeping Woman? He laughed out loud, swinging his zippered notebook from his little finger.

At this juncture, I think, no serious evocation of landscape. What else will serve?

Let me see. Orestes can give her ice-cream at the café. (It must be Summer. O.'s sabbatical year will just have begun.) A mild dusk. The awnings that close me in won't be needed. It will divert her to sit in full view of the populace—the grande dame of the island, already on such jolly terms with the newcomer.

He will talk.

"I was born 35 years ago in Asia Minor of Greek parents. My father, a goatherd, fell in love with a beautiful etc. Dead of cancer. Poverty. New York. Mother remarried, lives in Texas. A step-father, ~~a half-brother~~

No. Avoid plunging stupidly into exposition. Let him be felt a bit. Let *her* be felt.

(Orson — Orestes. Now another name for Dora.)

And let *me* not be part of it. It's hard enough being O.'s brother in life, without sentencing myself to it in a book.

Maria
Psyche
Fifi (Serafina)
Kiki
(Pulcheria)
Artemis

~~Orestes~~

Little stream, have you petered out so soon?

This is my first prolonged exposure to the *town* of

Diblos (1800 souls). It has, I can report so far, a hotel & a café. In the hotel are 12 rooms, 2 baths, a manager in pyjamas morning and night, an energetic Italian-speaking maid named Chryssoula whose children— Yannis, Theodoros, Aphrodite, six all told—run errands & whose big black cat does not. Here at the café, the canvas, still rolled down, is flapping furiously. An umber heat pulses through it. My table lurches from side to side as I write, at one with the incomprehensible voices, rattle of beads, the click & screech of crockery. It is 4:00 of my 2nd day here, and of my 7th in Greece for as many years. I'd thought one of the first things to do would be to walk out to the House, but I haven't. Nor have I wanted in any way to 'use' my previous visit, or my connection with O. & Dora. The natives have shown, up to now, no glimmer of recognition.

5:30. The boat from Athens has come & gone. The awnings are rolled up. Nobody in sight. I could be giving thought to

5:45. The American girl, Lucy, from the N.'s lunch last week, was on the boat. I hadn't noticed her getting off. She seemed ominously glad to see a familiar face. Then: "But you're *working*, excuse me!"—leaving me with the choice of being amused by her view of the Writer as finer & nobler than the rest of us or being undone by the whole sorry banality of writing so much as a postcard in a public place. Anyhow, she couldn't join me. A luggage-bearing child led her off to a room taken, sight unseen. Will she be here long? I didn't ask. I am so cold to people. And keep forgetting that it's that, the coldness, the remoteness, that attracts them. If I were warmer, talked more, showed more interest, *felt* more interest—

To fit in somewhere:
(Dora) was constantly polite and respected, but Orestes had *time* for people, time to talk and show interest, to make his listeners feel that their minds were rare & flexible, time to welcome a stranger into the circle with some deft bit of nonsense from the speaker's well of inexhaustible friendliness. This kind of conversation finds its happiest expression in the dialogues of Plato, where for all Socrates' avowed humility it is certainly he who does the talking & remains the center of attention. The system worked like a charm at the waterfront café where a half dozen idle citizens would be held spellbound, hours on end, while (Dora) knitted. "How do you do it?" she asked one day.
"What do you mean? I like doing it," he said.
"How can you?" was on the tip of her tongue. Instead she returned to her ~~knitting~~ handiwork, head bowed in acknowledgment of her friend's superior humanity.
(The Greek restaurant in New York: a contrasting scene.)

17.vi.61
From the postoffice (no letters yet) a strange view of the Sleeping Woman, seen only by afternoon light until today. Barely recognizable, a collapsing tent of

whitish bluffs & uncertain distances; let Orestes see her that way just before (after?) the confrontation on the terrace.

Seen from the café, now, the Woman is more distinct: knee, belly, ribcage, breast (a shallow hemisphere) slung backwards to the long throat; a firm jutting chin, nose ditto; mouth shut, refusal of a kiss.

She gives the landscape an intense dreamlike quality. In the foreground, set low, an Italianate composition of peeling villa, cypress, palm, lemon trees, all green-black between the sky-colored water & the hills pale as clouds.

Even the narrow channel between island and mainland struck Orestes as emblematic. He thought of the "tight straits" of his early life.

18.vi.61
Along the quai are moored the little water-taxis, each shaded by a canopy of white cloth. This, on Dora's more stylish boat, had a border of scarlet fringe.

She sent the boat for Orestes the following afternoon. The young boatman
"Well, this has been very nice," said (Dora)—they were now speaking English. She gave him her hand, adding as if it meant nothing, "You wouldn't be a bridge fan?

He stared at her, thinking of ~~Hart Crane~~ water to be spanned.

"Or any card game. It helps to pass the time."

"Oh you know," cried Orestes joyously, understanding & savoring his conquest, "I have no talent for such things. I would play a diamond instead of a heart —is that what the suits are called?" He ended by noticing her smile. "Would you like me to play cards with you?" he said meekly.

She sent the boat for him the following afternoon. The young boatman, Kosta, knew him by sight. In those days before the tourists discovered (Diblos) every stranger was known, through someone's hospitable interrogation, within an hour of arrival.

(It's moving too quickly.)

(That same night) Orestes strolled the length of the waterfront to a taverna above the beach—from afar, a diamond blaze, a faint blare of song; once there, 8 tables, a central rectangle of earth, unshaded bulbs strung on wires. A whitewashed cube, windowless, in whose forehead burned the strongest bulb, completed the setting. Two couples sat at one table, two sailors at another. ~~Orestes~~ The music had stopped. O. nodded about politely, seated himself and ordered wine & cheese from the child who came stumbling out over an apron that covered him from chest to ankles.

Ah wait. Insert:

At a 3rd table sat a small, plump infant of a man, dashingly dressed, an Athenian on holiday, O. supposed in the moment it took to nod about & choose a table removed from the outsider. He seated himself, etc.

¶ A rhythmical grating, ominous & blurred, the needle in its groove, heralded the next selection. From the loudspeaker issued a splatter of twanging sounds, a melody any fragment of which seemed feverish but whose final effect was one of tragic lassitude. A voice put words to it:

> "In Trikala where two alleys meet
> They murdered Sahavlià . . ."

(Or find other words. Love & Betrayal. Make them up?)

One of the sailors rose to dance. He snapped fingers, leapt, dipped, never looked up. Above him, counterwise to his movements, a lightbulb slowly revolved. When the dance ended, the small plump man, who had come unnoticed to Orestes' table, asked permission to sit down.

The Enfant Chic.

He is forever pursing his pale mouth and rolling his pale eyes. A silken swag of hair, a lightly-pitted face like the moon's. The rest of him vanishes into his new clothes; the white collar stands out from his ears, only his knuckles show below the pink cuffs. In talking, he spreads out his hands & the two middle fingers stay glued together as on fashion dummies. He would be, oh, 40. One thinks at first he is a photographer; he leers at one, mimes the snapping of a picture. Is he mad? His manner changes. He asks if one knows an Athens shop called l'Enfant Chic. No, no, no, he does not own it. No, no, he doesn't buy his clothes there, hahaha. The outspread hand flattens upon his heart. Ze suis, moi, l'Enfant Seek. Actually his name is Yannis, as whose isn't, and he runs a shop of his own here called Tout pour le Sport.

That's not going to work. There's no place for the Enfant Chic in this story. Yet he lives here. ~~Orson~~ Orestes could have to reckon with him, & for O. he'd be a rather different person, able to speak his own language, dispense with those airs of complicity, of knowing more than he tells, put on by his utter ignorance—of me, of English, even of French—like one more piece of smart clothing.

I touched one glass too many with other revellers, & cannot account for a big blue bruise below my hip.

What one *can* use is the poetry of the night, the lights running across black water toward us from the mainland, the music dwarfed, though at top volume, by the immense starry silences around it. To swim then: one's limbs, stippled with phosphorescence, bringing to mind—to my mind—ectoplasm, the genie conjured up out of oneself, floating & sporting, performing all that's asked of it before it merges at last into the dark chilled bulk of its master's body stumbling over stones to sleep.

19.vi.61

"Come in here." She opened the door. Orestes followed her into a sunny library. Lamplight revealed

Near the bright window, but lamplit as if for a faint increase of warmth, a shrunken old man lay on a chaise-longue. A blanket covered him to the waist. "Tasso," she said, "we have a guest."

A second figure replaced a book in shelves near the door and turned. He was a handsome, heavy man of about thirty, dressed in a sheer white shirt & white trousers. "This is my son Byron," said (Dora). And in another voice, "There is my husband."

Orestes gazed at her with admiration. He had talked so much about himself the previous day, and only now realized that she, too, must have a life worth hearing about.

The old man, holding O.'s hand, stared up at him from over a full white and yellow beard. "Siate voi il poeta?" he breathed reverently.

"Oui," said Orestes. "You must forgive me, I do not speak French."

Byron ~~on whose face a look of petulance~~ walked over, looking amused. "My father paints, you know. He terribly enjoys meeting a fellow intellectual. We get few visitors of any sort nowadays."

"Solitude is the price the artist pays," said Orestes, mechanically rhyming.

"I would prefer to pay it in Paris," said Byron.

"And I in ~~Rapallo~~ Fiesole," said the old man. "For 32 years I have not left Greece. But small countries make delightful prisons." Although he still had hold of Orestes' hand, he seemed to have mastered his initial emotion.

We should have had a glimpse of Orestes before this—at the café?

He was a slight, graceful

a spare, nimble man in sandals, white trousers, & a white drip-dry shirt through which his undershirt and lean darkening shoulders could be seen. Already balding, his square brow gleamed like beeswax above ~~brown deepset animated heavylidded~~ triangular brown eyes. He rarely wore the sunglasses in his pocket. On his left wrist, a bracelet of paler skin; he had left his watch off, for the sake of an even tan. Below the moustache of a 'sharpie', his lips, thin & curveless, tinged with purple, appeared unexpressive in repose. He was at his best when talking. Presently, looking up from his book, he

20.vi.61

Something too odd has happened. The Enfant Chic knows me. He has a photograph of me.

The coincidence tells me I must face up to the 'reality'—actual events & people—behind my story. How much to conceal, how much to invent? The name Orson, which still, to my ear, sounds *truer* than Orestes, has had to go already. But who he is (Orson/Orestes)— and by the same token, who I am—ah, that I keep on evading.

At least I understand the E. C.'s picture-snapping pantomime at the taverna. He had recognized me, he knew I was Orson's brother. ("Couldn't the Tourist Police have given him your name?" asked Lucine later, missing the point: we had different names, were only

*half*-brothers—she found it strangely difficult to grasp.)
Anyhow, today, when I looked in on the Enfant's lair
of fishnet, handwoven skirts, sandals, postcards & shells,
he was ready for me. He had the snapshot to show.

He asked eagerly where Orson was & wouldn't believe I couldn't tell him. He had known O., then? Yes,
yes. He had known him. Z'étais grande
ami de maison. Próto—avant. Après,
pas. Tu comprends? I understood
mainly how Orson would have loathed
him on sight. Small wonder I was never
taken to call. The E. C. admits that
he doesn't remember me from 7 years
ago, but at that time he had had no shop, he hadn't
(adjusting imaginary furs) needed to work.

The E. C. can
be present
at Orestes'
1st visit to
the House?

But how did he get the snapshot?

Oh yes, & as I am leaving, in a tone of benevolent
confidence: Tell your brother to stay away from Diblos
—ne pas revenir, O. K.?

I guess I was right. The Enfant Chic has a place in
the story.

Leaving the shop, they shook hands. Orestes was
revolted to feel
revolted but not surprised to feel his palm tickled
by the proprietor's moist, long-nailed finger.

On the street I met Lucy, or Lucine as she turns
out to be called (name misheard at the N.'s). Still in
state of mild shock, suggested swim. She considered at

length, then said yes with air of an earnest, headstrong
10 year old. Marvelous water, marvelous air. She
doesn't know the N.'s any better than I do. Thought
her mother had gone to school with Mrs N. She seems
independent. (Parents think she's traveling with chums.)
She must paint—funny little hands stained orange &
blue, nails bitten.

A more formal opening: O.'s arrival in Athens.
No sooner had Orestes

The snapshot seemed at first to show Orestes &
his brother, in profile, face to face. But a closer look revealed that Orestes was there only in plaster effigy, as if
transformed by something in the young, inexperienced
the barely formed, mindless features of the other.

22.vi.61
Dusk of another day. Café awnings rolled up. Ouzo
ordered.
Earlier, thinking I'd walk out to the House, I
passed the beach. Lucine sketching, oblivious to the 4
young men not far off who grind their bellies into the
sand & fix her with burning eyes. The Enfant Chic oil-
ing his plump limbs in the center of a huge blue & white
towel—the Greek flag? He has a few young men of his
own. "Bon zour, où vous allez madenant?"—and
when I don't stop, makes elaborate gestures 1st in my
direction, then towards the distant, invisible House.
His friends, too, waved & smiled—ah, they know me

from that night at the taverna. Angry, I did a childish thing: branched off the path—the House would keep— and struck out up a wooded slope in the direction of, well, nowhere at all. Fields, olive groves, *lots* of burrs. And were the E. C. and his friends deceived? Ha! Not likely.

To reconsider:

1) Orestes has come to (Diblos) for a week. Meets (Dora). The card game, etc.

2) Back in Athens, he runs into (Byron) on the street & hears that his father has died.

3) In reply to his letter of sympathy Dora, now left alone—Byron works in Athens—impulsively offers Orestes the cottage on her property.

Yes. So we see him in residence by early fall. They can have all winter to reach the point at which O.'s brother finds them when he comes in April.

But must the brother really be in the story? If he is, a terrific lot of back history will have to be put in. The Greek father, the American father, even the old godfather, Arthur Orson (who might be useful, though, in New York—someone for Dora to turn to). How much I'd rather there weren't this complexity! I wanted a tale light as air, lightly breathed out, 2 or 3 figures only, in clear, unexpected colors. And now look.

They needn't *be* brothers! Wouldn't that solve everything?

24.vi.61

A Monday. Father's seasonal letter. When was I
returning, money not grown on trees, enclosed check
the last. "Mother joins in love to you & Orson." Let
them think we are together. I need time here, now; the
book is starting to take hold.

Yesterday noon, on the bus to the monastery where
a festival (panegyri) was being held, Lucine rambled
on in her soft sleepwalking way. The Greek boys, she
didn't know if she liked them, they followed her about
so. She must be almost as young as she looks to expect
one to care for her trivial plight. Nobody, that is, has
done her wrong. Still, I spent most of the day at her
side, pretending a protectiveness not too surprisingly
felt by early evening when, full of wine, we reeled the 6
kilometers downhill into the moonrise.

"Have you shown your paintings anywhere?"

"No. Have you had anything published?"

"A few things."

"That's too bad. I think everyone should be un-
known."

It may have been then that I kissed her.

Orestes: I have had more experience than you.
(Name): Must it follow that " " " leads to wisdom?

26.vi.61

I want to say something about loneliness and dis-
tance. Already I'm not lonely enough. There is L.,
there is the Enfant Chic, there is a body named Giorgios

who asked me for a cigarette on the beach and said "You good man," as he went off with two. In the hotel, there is Chryssoula. However slightly they know me, I find I must avoid them if I am to accomplish anything.

This morning I wrote letters in my room's airless, viewless heat. Chryssoula exclaimed with dismay, seeing me emerge; she had thought I was on the beach, otherwise she would have kept me company! Now, this afternoon, I have picked my way along what can't be called a path, out beyond the edge of town (direction opposite from that of the House). Here it is wild & stony, there are goats high up behind me, some savage green flies. I've had to cross a gulley blackened with human excrement. It may be where the fishermen come to swim, though the water looks unclean & choppy, and nobody is in sight.

Naturally one would prefer the sweep & style of the port, to have a place among the tiny foreground figures (netmenders, women with jars, checkerplayers, coffeedrinkers) beyond whom the lagoon, its silk-pale perspective, leads to the symbolic sleeper—one would prefer that to the awful spot I'm in now. Yet here, in spite of flies, smells, nowhere comfortable to sit, I am somehow able to dwell on that other scene as never before. The region the Sleeping Woman dominates is Troezen—l'aimable Trézène, Phaedra's last home—

not that (Dora) is Orestes' stepmother, but he himself can wax articulate over the ambiguous emotions each rouses in the other.

A sudden attack of diarrhea took me to the water's

edge. Instead of climbing back to my rock, or heading back to town for medicine, I went on to the next cove where the channel is narrowest & the water roughest. Here was standing some kind of absurd house, or shed, half built *into* the water, a mess of rotting boards & plaster. A truly hideous smell came from it. I thought I was dreaming: the steps, the doorless threshold, the nearby rocks, were all spattered & stained with blood. One felt it dripping from within, into the current— some of it fresh enough to have been this morning's. I gathered finally that I had found the slaughterhouse. I'd never thought of islands' having slaughterhouses! There was a dog, even, yellow, filthy, cringing among remnants of God knows what. A 2nd attack of cramps kept me there, unable to move. Like blood my own excrement ran glittering down the rocks into the sea which feinted & struck back, hissing. Further out— there are meant to be no sharks in these waters—I'm sure I saw fins.

Now, back in the hotel. It is evening, a soft, sweet breeze fills my room. Chryssoula sent out for pills. They are working. But I remain grateful for what I have seen. I have been shown something that my story needs.

Years ago, in his lecture on Darwin & the Poetry of Science, Orestes made much of the chemical affinities of blood and seawater. If he, with his passion for dialectic, ever takes that walk, will he find in the slaughterhouse an antithesis to the serene harbor view, or a synthesis of that view & its beholder?

Something to be concealed *by* the story, by the

writing—as in *Phèdre* where the overlay of prismatic verse deflects a brutal, horrible action.

30.vi.61
The dream continues. Days have passed. I am sitting on the deck of the N.'s caïque which swooped down upon Diblos Friday like a Machine, gathered us up (L. & me) and swept us off to Epidauros where we have now sat through 2 nights of Drama with nothing but foam rubber between ourselves & antiquity. On our return to Diblos this afternoon we shall find Mrs N.'s telegrams warning us of the evacuation.

It was dazzling. The child, L.'s landlady's grandson, discovered us first, on the beach at noon. Within minutes he'd been joined by 2 of Chryssoula's children from the hotel. In unison they delivered the big news— our friends from Athens had arrived, were looking for us!—before a rapidly forming chorus of beach-boys wearing, like identical costumes, an obligation to share the news at once with their Leader. We ourselves scarcely registered what was up, before some of them were sprinting toward his shop.

We slung our clothes into towels and followed, conscious of the town's impatience. On the waterfront, Lucine stopped: we were still in bikinis, she'd been scolded once already by the Tourist Police for wearing an immodest garment off the beach. Precious moments elapsed while Adam & Eve covered their nakedness before entering His presence who had brought them together in the 1st place.

Mr N. was pacing the quai. The blue & white caïque with its linen awnings and mahogany gangplank lay creaking in its sleep beside him. He is about 60, bronzed, black-browed, silver-fringed; he had on a very elegant pale gray suit, white moccasins, a foulard at his throat. "Here you are, splendid," he hailed us. "But aren't you ready? weren't you expecting us?" Explanations; amazement; the telegraph service deplored. "No matter. My wife says we're ahead of time. Run along, put some things together & meet us at your convenience. Here or at the café—or in one of those shops" —for we had just glimpsed Mrs N. waving from the Enfant Chic's doorway. Her husband motioned her to stay where she was, incidentally sparing her L.'s finger-nails & my unshaven face. We made bright signals back, then followed Mr N.'s instructions.

At the hotel (L.'s room is 5 minutes up the hill) we hesitated. It was a moment for consultation. To what end? Had we been sleeping together, we would have had to agree on how to act for the next 48 hours, to which of the numberless half-tones between frankness & artifice we should try to tune ourselves. How charming such moments can be! As it was, I merely said I wasn't sure I felt like going on an excursion, & did she? The question baffled her, she knitted her brows at the sky. Now that the N.'s were here, had we any choice? So it was decided. I mentioned her nails. Within the hour we had left our sparse baggage aboard & were pushing our way through the onlookers that clogged the Enfant Chic's doorway.

He had sent out for coffee. Mrs N. (sleeveless lilac dress, sandals) had drunk hers & was wielding an honest-to-goodness fan of stiff silver paper. She rose, greeted Lucine with a kiss and me with a peculiar ironic gaze that trilled above her easy manners like an oboe above a string quartet. I understood it better later. At the time, it seemed, once again, that we *ought* to have been lovers, L. & I, in order further to feel that with charming, civilized people like the N.'s no pretense to the contrary would be called for. The Enfant gave me his left hand. Our coffees were cool, we drank them on our feet. A merry rapid conversation in Greek was pursued onto the blinding whitewashed steps. Our exit causing the teenage chorus to withdraw somewhat, the E. C. had to raise his voice to show how well he knew his smart guests from Athens. One final sally from Mrs N. made him turn & cover his face with a dimpled hand. The audience broke into laughter. "Really!" Mr N. murmured, taking his wife's arm as we walked away.

Lucine: What was the joke?

Mrs N. (smiling): Nothing. Pure nonsense.

Mr N.: Nonsense indeed. My impossible wife said it had been a pleasure, an honor, to visit that gentleman's boutique, and that she fully intended to come back & spend thousands of drachmas there—only she would have to come alone, without any *men* to distract him from making a sale.

Mrs N. (with profound conviction): But you saw, he was thrilled! It made his day!

On the caïque—which is quite grand inside: fox-
fur rugs on the divans, & French pictures, & a crew of 5
—we changed into bathing-suits and ate lobster salad
on deck. We had gotten under way.

The meaning of the look Mrs N. had given me was
duly, ever so diffidently & amusedly, explained. They'd
just learned from the Enfant Chic that I was Orson's
brother, and were astonished. So was I. I couldn't believe that they hadn't known, that Dora's letter asking
them to be nice to me had described me simply as a
'young friend' of hers. Well, the kaleidoscope has
turned with a vengeance.

They were now slightly on guard. I was made to
feel that I should have found a way to enlighten them
upon our first meeting—despite there having been
other guests at lunch and the N.'s not having opened
the subject.

However, here I was. Perhaps something could be
learned from me.

"You see," said Mrs N. uncrossing her smooth
brown legs to hand me coffee, "while we're old friends
of Dora's—Akis especially, I am younger" (as if one
hadn't noticed)—"we left, a week after her husband's
death, for 2 years in London & Paris. I am French by
birth, and Akis was an adviser to the X. Y. Z. You can
imagine our amazement when letters from Athens began to pour in, telling us that she had gone to America
with this man, with your brother who I'm sure must be
perfectly charming (I've seen the film he worked on
twice, and he was also a great friend of some people we

know intimately). All I mean," very apologetically, "is that, absurd as it must sound to an American, Dora had a position here in society. Her father was an ambassador, her aunts were ladies-in-waiting to the old Queen. Her husband belonged to one of our best provincial families. Also, Dora had reached a certain age. One wouldn't have cast her in the role of Anna Karenina."

"You exaggerate," said Mr N. with a smile. "Remember, she was free to do as she liked." Then, turning to me, severely: "She worked as a governess for over a year. Did you know that?"

I nodded. He went on, speaking in a legato tenor voice lovely to hear. Things were different in America. Married women worked, enjoyed independence unheard of in Greece where no husband would permit, etc.

Mrs N. (interrupting): But you're talking as if we knew for certain that Dora had married this man. The rumor may be totally unfounded.

Mr N.: You're hopeless, Nicole. Of course they are married. She has been how long in America? Six years? Without a passport she'd have been deported after 6 months.

Mrs N.: Is it true? I'll have to marry an American if I'm to have my last wish in life?

I: What's that?

Mrs N.: My last wish is to die while playing canasta in Atlanta, Georgia, the home of Scarlett O'Hara.

Mr N.: It's too much, one can discuss nothing with you.

A pause. Mrs N. (animated): No! I want to say

that I can understand Dora. Heavens! Who doesn't want to be American today? Look what dollars are doing for this country. Suddenly we have roads, hotels— ça fait impression, vous savez.

Here Lucine, curled up with her chin in a cushion, made a remark (her own?) to the effect that, yes, America was buying Europe, country by country. The next victim was clearly Greece. L. felt lucky to have come here in time.

We discussed it a while, skimming the sapphire depths of the immense subject. The N.'s wouldn't exactly admit that Greece was being spoiled—"How can you spoil *this*?" with a sweep of the hand that took in sea & sun & the approaching heights of Mycenae—but did grant that a certain quaint charm was being sacrificed. For this we could thank the Greek-Americans. They (or a faction that poured money into Greece and so had influence in high places) were responsible for the virtual disappearance of tavernas in Athens. It gave them, the G.-A.'s, a bad name when other Americans saw a pair of men get up & dance together. They'd even tried to keep the bouzoukia music—to which such dances are done—off the radio, etc. Mr N. was the first to recall that Orson fitted into the category of Greek-Americans, as for that matter did I, despite my appearance. "You understand, I don't speak of intellectuals," he said, as if there were other Greek-American intellectuals besides O. Well, there may be; nothing's impossible.

It strikes me as I write that this national theme

could be most expressively illuminated by the story of
Orestes & (Dora)—the one coming to Greece athirst
for his past, unaware of how it is his coming, and that of
others like him, that will in the end obliterate what he
has come for; the other asking nothing better than to be
changed, to take on the fancied independence & glamor
of the American woman. *Remember this.*

Mr N. said unexpectedly, "I knew your brother.
In fact it was I who introduced him to Dora."

His wife stared in consternation. "Akis, it's true?
You never told me so!"

Mr N. (winking at L. & me): If you say I never
told you, then you must be right, because you are always right. However, you'll recall my going to Diblos
overnight not long before Tasso's death. He wanted
some slight changes in his will. As the boat wasn't
crowded, I sat on deck. Your brother was sitting nearby, reading *Antony & Cleopatra*. I took him for a student.
We talked for 2 hours. He had all kinds of lively &, to
me, original ideas. Tasso, I thought, would be diverted
by him. So I asked him to the house for lunch the next
day. In fact I left him there when I went to catch the
afternoon boat. That's all.

Mrs N.: That's all! But you're mad! Invited him
to lunch? Someone Dora had never met!

Mr N.: What do you mean? I bring strangers
home to lunch all the time.

Mrs N.: Watch out, from now on, that I don't
marry one of them!

She brought her large blue eyes to bear, humorously, upon me. I had been wondering in what previous life I'd encountered the N.'s—or where they had found themselves. It was in the pages of Proust. Addressing each other, they shared with the Duke & Duchess of Guermantes that same ironic consciousness of an audience.

Mr N. (patiently): Do I have to explain that there was no question, during lunch, of Dora's marrying our friend's brother? They need never have seen him again.

Mrs N.: And you, did you see him again? It's fascinating, this glimpse into one's husband's life!

Mr N.: I did not see him again. Nor did I see Tasso again until 6 weeks later when we went to his funeral.

Mrs N.: I remember! He was barefoot in his coffin. There was an asphodèle in his lapel.

Mr N.: I beg your pardon, it was in his hand.

Mrs N.: I beg yours. In one hand he held his edition of Dante. The other hand was empty.

Mr N.: You see, she's always right.

I still prefer my version of Orestes' & (Dora)'s meeting. Can I use the N.'s in my book? As Lucine said when they'd gone below to take naps, "They're funny."

L. is funny enough, if less useful. I've sat beside her both nights at Epidauros. She watched the plays with a concentration I'd have thought impossible to muster out of doors. The more glorious the natural setting, the less I care for the human figure. At Epidauros it was like a ballet of fleas on a round, lamplit table. When the gods finally came, I wanted them to be 40 feet tall.

What were they doing but the *Oresteia*! A weird
neo-Wagnerian prelude, tubas & strings, offstage. The
actors unmasked. The watchman cries φῶς! into the
afterglow (the first & virtually last intelligible word)
and soon the stage is flooded with artificial dawn.

The *Agamemnon* was familiar; the two plays that
followed, not. I've been reading them in a translation
bought yesterday. They are very strange. For instance:

*Agamemnon*—a Chorus made up of old men, comi-
cally powerless. They wring hands, complain, sympa-
thize, disapprove. Nothing more.

*The Libation-Bearers*—a Chorus of young women.
They have considerably more influence. Not that they
*do* anything, yet they are able to persuade the Nurse to
have Aegisthus arrive unarmed, thus ensuring his death.

*The Eumenides*—Chorus of Furies (Kindly Ones)
which totally dominates stage & action. Orestes enters
holding, instead of a sword, a leafy branch—his mind
no longer adamant but diffuse, perishable, rustling in
a wind none of the others can feel. The furies *possess* him.
Only at the end, with the intervention of Divine Wisdom (Athena) do they become civil & courteous,
marching off with their judges. Each casts two shadows,
one orange, one green. Verdict: O. shall go free; the
Kindly Ones shall be given shrines.

This resolution moved me. The gods alone can
change turmoil to peace, hatred to love.

Orestes might reply: I refuse to believe that. The
tensions within man's soul, within society, must effect
the miracle.

How wrong he will be to think so!

Throughout, buzzing of insects, buzzing of time-exposures. Hushed explications from the N.'s.

Lucine's attentiveness. The unfolding story must have come as a surprise. When she gathered that Orestes was going to kill his mother, she gave a short gasp, her eyes were sparkling with tears. She impressed me as belonging there, her short curls & clenched hands, uncreasable white dress knotted at the shoulder, there under the rising moon. She was in a sense far more Greek than the N.'s.

I may not see her after tonight.

A car drove us from the theatre to Nauplion where the caïque was already moored. Town jammed. 100's of torches streaming along jetties & up hillsides in honor of the drama festival. We sat at an outdoor taverna. Mr N. thought of going into the kitchen to order our food. L. accompanied him.

Mrs N. began by saying she had gone to a Swiss school with L.'s mother, that they were an "excellent" California family—"Remind me another time to ask you what that means!" They had hoped she would look out for the child this summer, which she was glad to do.

I said that Lucine's having money explained her air of poverty.

"Oh, they have money. That doesn't prejudice me against them, does it you? Who knows, our daughter may go to America one day. Stranger things have happened."

Where was her daughter now?

"With her grandmother in France. She's charming if I do say so myself. Just 16. A pity you can't meet her."

Her tone, pure Guermantes, told me she meant precisely the opposite. Having decided long ago that Orson was an adventurer bent on marrying a rich wife, but never having had occasion to wither him by saying so to his face, Mrs N. was finding it appropriate & economical—2 birds, 1 stone—to act as if he and I were the same person.

I could have told her then that my father had money, too, even if O. preferred to be proud & poor. Instead, I wanted to know if Lucine had written to the N.'s about me.

"Tell *me* something," Mrs N. countered, giving her marvelous imitation of devouring curiosity. "How old are you?" Then: "I thought so. Along with having a nice face, you're clever for your age. If you're as young as you say, you'll remember what it was like to be still younger—to be *her* age. The age at which whoever one meets makes an impression. Her character is still being formed. It's a temptation, I admit, to add some little touch of one's own. You've added yours, in any case, from the first day."

Several things needed to be said right off. But Mr N. & Lucine were back, a waiter following with glasses & wine.

I wanted to explain about Orson—that there were differences between us, which had gone so far as to be dramatized by our present ~~coolness~~ estrangement. But Mrs N. had given me to feel that he & I stood or fell

together. In her eyes at least, *he* had taken advantage of
Dora's age, *I* was taking advantage of L.'s youth. Was
there no age that couldn't be taken advantage of? Well,
there was Mrs N.'s who would, for another 5 years if not
for the rest of her life, turn everything to her own profit.

Both her implications, actually, were unjust. I
would have liked to correct them.

We began talking about the plays. I said tenta-
tively—the words were Orson's, not mine—that the
Greek myths had become more & more literary, that
indeed, if it hadn't been for Freud, we should have no
key to their shocking power.

Mr N. observed that in Europe Freud was passé,
Europe had gone beyond Freud.

"Where has it gone?" asked L., really wanting to
know.

Mrs N. (breaking bread): Don't ask him that, I
*think* he could tell you! I *think* it has been written down
in 500 books of varying thickness which Akis will lend
you, or I will—on condition that you mislay them one
by one.

Her tone was infectious. Having set out to defend
Orson, I made gentle fun of him instead. It was fascinating (I said) how deeply O., as both a Greek & a
'modern man', longed to enter that world of myth. For
instance, it had never been enough just to be on plain
bad terms with his stepfather (my father). Orson
wasn't happy until he could see him as Aegisthus &
Mother as Clytemnestra, instead of an ordinary well-off
Texas oil man (Mrs N. take note) and his Greek-born

wife. By the same token Orson, in loving Dora, may have loved particularly the idea of her being 'old enough to be his mother'. He had been analyzed (met the Sphinx); here he was in Europe. Between the Dowager Queens of Thebes and Diblos there wasn't much to choose.

I still had hoped to show Mrs N. how little of a fortune-hunter Orson was. Her face told me I had succeeded too well; she would think of him henceforth as seriously unbalanced.

L.'s face showed something else. She's taken not my words so much as my tone of voice. Later, under the full moon, she asked what had been wrong, why I'd talked that way. "You sounded like the N.'s, making fun of everything, you know? Are you like them?" Meaning, O God, what? that I was false & superficial, that my heart was withered in my breast? No, I was not like them, I told her, & closed that fearful little mouth with a kiss.

Still at table, L. asked where Orson was now. I'd begun to think no one would, & drained my wineglass before speaking.

"I'm not sure. In New York, the last I heard."

"No," said Mr N., "your brother is in Athens. He telephoned my office last week."

Sensation.

Mr N.: It has its pathetic side. He's under the impression that he has a claim upon Dora's property, specifically upon a small cottage behind the house, which he says she gave him. There was no legal agreement, I assure you. The cottage was never Dora's to give. Under Tasso's will, the entire property goes to Byron after her death. Your brother is asking us, nevertheless, to write to Dora, and to Byron, how shall I say? sounding them out—

Lucine (rich girl, identifying): Even though they're married, he wouldn't be able—

Mrs N.: They are married? Still!

Mr N.: Yes of course. But we have no Code Napoléon in Greece, whereby a man is entitled to his wife's estate.

Mrs N.: It's true? You married me for love, Akis?

Mr N. (pressing her hand): You see through me like clear glass.

I: But then you've seen Orson?

Mr N.: As a friend of Dora's I thought it tactfuller to let a younger man in our office handle the case.

Mrs N.: He's not going to court!

Mr N.: Ah no. He's asking where he stands, that's all.

L. (to me): You didn't know he was in Greece? Don't you write each other?

I begged her not to worry, O. & I would find each other soon enough. That was the time to bring up the famous letter of last year in N. Y.—I'd broken faith, was no longer the person I had been, I had "sided against him." The N.'s I don't think would have believed me, or if so, would have been further prejudiced against Orson. One doesn't *write* letters like that! One certainly doesn't try to answer them.

(In any case, O. can only just have arrived in Greece. Good Lord, it's his sabbatical again. Seven years!)

Mrs N. came oddly near the mark. "You're not close to your brother, then?"

I shrugged it off. We'd grown up apart, 15 years' difference in age, etc.

"But you *became* close."

"Yes. Well, only here in Greece. At Dora's."

"So—" throwing up her hands at the devious ways of life—"you *are* Dora's friend after all! Something told me!"

"Dora told you," I said smiling.

"Perhaps you've even taken her side—brothers have been *known* to quarrel over women. Akis, tu écoutes? It's dramatic!"

(With people like the N.'s, evidently, I could make light of O. But in my story he must be kept fine & serious. Which means that I must keep sprinkling my sandy heart with that view of him.)

This was our 2nd & last night. The N.'s had booked rooms in a hotel on shore, as being more comfortable than the caïque. I said goodnight on the street, I was going to walk a bit. At 1 end of town a wide white path led round tall cliffs, blue, pulverized in moonlight. L. caught up with me there. Once I'd kissed her she seemed to relax. I led her back to the hotel, my arm around her. Outside her room, kissed her again. I didn't want anything to happen.

Ouf!

I've been writing all morning, my whole body aches. The others are due back from Mycenae. Since I stayed behind, they can tell me what I missed. The plan, as of yesterday, is to sail for Diblos after lunch, pick up some clothes, & move on to other islands for a week or 2 of Pleasure. We are all so congenial, said Mrs N., it was a shame to separate. (Is she really Mme Verdurin?) Lucine is so passive, any suggestion automatically excludes an alternative. She said it sounded lovely. I said I was expecting letters which would have to decide for me. It will be NO.

Diblos. Past midnight. I've seen L. off on the caïque.

Her face in moonlight, gray & mild, as if about to ~~administer~~ receive an anesthetic.

Before that, in the empty street. Her bags packed, the N.'s already aboard. I stepped back from her, trying to reason. She'd given up her room. I couldn't take her to mine.

face in moonlight, grown transparent, a darkness bleeding through lips & eyes. The cricket's gauze-dry

"Yes I see."

I said something.

She: You don't want it to happen. You're writing your book, you don't need anything else.

I said we would meet again. Athens, America . . .

Eaten by light      silver maw

The moon had risen and drunk the water

"I thought the Greek boys weren't human beings,

were animals really, thinking just of their bodies. It seemed so selfish—" Whispering.

She was right. The soul's selfishness was worse. The thirst for pattern, whether that of words on a page or stresses in the universe. The hubris that invents tragedy for the glory of undergoing it. As I saw O., Lucine saw me.

In my arms once more. Take me somewhere. I don't care. Please.

She was so young, she thought that to feel love meant that it must be returned. My heart went out to her. My flesh as well.

Neither cold nor hot, the moonlight had the flimsiness of gauze, the intensity of frost. It was a gas inhaled

> Holding my hand for comfort
>> inhale this gas
>> made by the cricket's voice
> Acting on ~~dark bl~~ indigo oxygen
>>> blind I go !

3 a.m. Impossible to sleep.

An opening. Orestes arrives at the Acropolis by full moon, only to have the whistle blow & the gates barred to him.

I could have sailed with them. She thought I would, up to the last.

I had taken her to some rocks above the path to the slaughterhouse.

1.vii.61

At last, the House.

I am sitting on pine-needles overlooking the smaller cove, the one we didn't bathe in. 50 yards away, the House faces across darker water to the mainland. It is, I imagine, 'Othonian' in style, with balconies, an empty niche, all pleasantly run down. It has shrunken over the years, or else the surrounding trees —eucalyptus, mimosa, cypress—have grown to disproportionate height.

The 'garden' was, is, paved with dirt, one of those that so often adjoins a 19th cent. plastered house. Trees, benches, marble fragments, the table, the geranium-urns stand up from the flat ground like pieces of scenery. A plate on a bench. One recognizes it not from life but from productions of Chekhov. One came out of the front door onto a kind of stage apron, a squarish terrace which was in fact the roof of the cistern—can that be right? Beyond it, rose the tips of small cypresses planted below; one could reach out and all but touch them. They, too, are higher now, but the flat empty space they protect still catches & holds the eyes. A 10 or 12 foot drop. Across the water: the slopes of the lemon groves, like a modern 'textured' hanging done in green & yellow wools.

Most of the action took place, had to, here on the terrace. Lunch, tea, Orson at his typewriter, Dora sewing. I close my eyes to see before me that recurring rubbery dessert of cornstarch & boiled milk & sugar, concocted for me alone by D. who said it would do

good. I could get through a few mouthfuls each meal;
after 4 days half of it was still left, hardening, a jellyfish
in sun. At the meal's end Kosta would come for instructions before taking the boat to town. Maritsa, their
soiled child toddling in her wake, would clear the table,
dish by dish. One by one we too rose & strolled off. Last
of all, the dog Kanella (Cinnamon). An act ending in a
theatre where there is no curtain.

Chryssoula had known Kosta & Maritsa; they
have moved to Athens.

It is there on the ~~moonlit~~ terrace that (Dora) confronts Orestes on his return from the lemon groves. At
dawn. She has sat up all night.

Entering the house: a large square hall, staircase
of dark wood. A window on the landing, some clear
panes, others of green or amber, making it all the harder
to see the old man's paintings. We had to take them
outdoors where they showed, I fear, dismally in the
live radiance. Dried blues & oranges, villas, vases,
women setting tables, windows onto the sea. Blossoms
pressed in a History of Impressionism.

Orestes cannot understand why his brother is so
touched by them—his own tastes run to Michelangelo,
Grunewald, the monumental, the metaphysical. Pi-
casso's Guernica. Have him ask, when they are alone,
"Why, (Name), should Tasso's paintings move you so?"

The reply to be carefully phrased, for here we
touch an essential point. "Perhaps because they *are* so
slight. They will not ~~change ask~~ command anybody to
change his life"—O. having quoted Rilke in the Athens
museum.

(Dora gives the brother a little harbor scene as they are leaving.)

Also downstairs: the salon—furniture under sheets, a marble mantel; the library—windowseats, Morris chairs, a gas heater, a Revue des Deux Mondes of 1936 with a dozen pages cut. Out in back: the well, the oven, the servants' quarters and, further off, Orestes' cottage. *His* cottage. *His* rock-garden. *His* private cove. How proud & happy it made him! Two whitewashed rooms paved with hexagonal terracotta, interspersed with square black, tiles. Rush chairs. A low, wide window. His marble *trouvaille* on the sill. The table strewn with papers, dictionaries. His life-mask, plaster painted dull red, hanging above. Two wooden beds, woven striped coverings. The pillow Mother embroidered for him—neon-pink & yellow flowers on black—which looked so sad, so cheap in Houston but was suddenly at home here

—for although she was by now thoroughly American, (Eleni's) hands still did what they had been taught to do in her childhood.

All this to be recalled in idyllic contrast to the apartment Orestes & Dora take in New York.

A name for O.'s brother: Sandy.

Look! A figure is walking out onto the terrace: no one I have ever seen. He turns round, speaks, is joined by a girl in toreador pants. Why, this will be my "Byron." He has overstayed the weekend.

He is deeply tanned, more gracefully built than

the real Byron—than mine, I mean. A libertine?! And his hair is turning gray.

If Sandy ever returns to the House, he can think, "That was my youth, where it bloomed." Will he need to recall his illness?

Once the buds opened, the red blossoms kept their shape for days & days, without perceptibly maturing . . .

I am so sleepy now. Slow bright tears of gum encrust a section of ~~mauve~~ bark, brownish-mauve, like mauve-brown bark, like rouge on a negress.

As they were leaving, (Dora) gave Sandy a little oil sketch of red geraniums.

2.vii.61

The Enfant Chic pauses, passing the café, to welcome me back. Mrs N. he pronounces *sarmante*. I smile & nod. But Mazmaselle Lucine, where is she? Gone. Then, like a cat pouncing: And your brother? I reply without hesitation: à New-York.

Seeing the Enfant reminds me, one of his beach friends, Giorgios, practised English on me today. Where are you from? Are you married? How old are you? Why not married? What do you earn a month? What does a car cost in America? a kilo of meat? one egg? It made, I thought, for a delightful conversation. I replied as I thought best, asked my own simple questions, & that was that. Neither knowing more than 50 words of the other's language, we were soon reduced to a friendly goodbye. (Who described talk between friends as the ticking of not quite synchronized clocks on the same shelf?)

Mrs N. shares George's peasant curiosity, but oh the elaborate web she must spin to trap each new fly of fact—while G. can do no better than to thread a single strand across one's path; one sees it from far off, & arranges to trip over it just to please him.

A month after the old painter's death, Orestes re-visited (Diblos). He called upon the widow in his soberest aspect, wearing neatly ironed pants & carrying a copy of his book on Euripides which she had asked to see. A preacherly note in his voice made (Dora) smile: it was for her to win *him* back to the world.

She carried the tea-tray onto the terrace. They were alone. Byron had stayed a week, was now again in Athens. Orestes knew this. They had drunk a coffee together, by chance, not long before. (Byron: "The estate must be settled, you know what these things are like"—then looked at O. with sudden doubtfulness.) B. drove off in a red sports car. Orestes had thought him quite dashing & friendly.

"Yes," she said without conviction. "We've spoiled him, though. He had the makings of a scholar."

Orestes glowed. She would have liked her son to resemble him!

She has not of course offered him the cottage in a letter. She does so now:

". . . come & go as you please . . . a place to work . . . each other's company if we want it; if not,

not. I can tick on alone here quite happily."

Pitched low, her voice proceeded from high in her throat and made her words sound insincere to one who didn't know that she had had an English governess.

Orestes' voice, answering her, shook. His ~~heart~~ pulses beat hard, as after some great physical exertion —a height scaled, blue waters glittering off into haze below. At that moment he had nothing to give her but his whole heart.

He fetches clothes & books from Athens. The cottage needs a new roof. He sleeps the 1st weeks in the big house.

September comes & goes, each week drier, bluer, a season flawlessly expiring toward storms. The question of their becoming lovers never arises; or arises once, later, too late to be answered simply.

He can have asked, concerned for her: Won't the townspeople talk?

She: They'll talk whatever I do.

(A scene in which the Enfant Chic is made to feel unwelcome.)

He would have become her lover, he would have been anything she wanted. Though Orestes, before this, had only loved younger women, he

(Dora), at 56, fulfilled a classic condition. She was 'old enough to be his mother'. Compared, however, to Eleni—grown puffy & ill-at-ease in unbecoming clothes, dependent on the oven that "thought for her" & the TV that "saw for her"—Dora's person had become refined, stylized, a garment that would always

be in style. Age could not wither her? It could, it had;
but the process was gentle & dignified, as with an
animal, and gave no offense.

Correspondingly:

Orestes' Latinate vocabulary (his emotions) now
gave way to authentic, simple forms: sea, sky, vine,
house, plate, stone, woman

: rock sea sun wine goat sky.

Each was enchanted by qualities appropriate to
the other's age. What energy & imagination Orestes
had! From this period dated a round table set up
permanently on the terrace, the repainting of the boat
(blue & white with a red-fringed awning); also, of
course, the cottage itself rejuvenated, beautified, his
dream come true. By spring a path that was more like
a rock garden connected it with the House. O. gathered
the plants on their walks. You would have thought that
he had never, that nobody had ever seen a flower before. The anemone. The grape hyacinth. The orchid
big as a bee. "Yes, yes," (Dora) had to keep saying,
"they are beautiful, you are right!"—laughing because it was true, they were. Still, to be made to say so
at every step—! He meanwhile had scrambled up an
embankment, waved, recited a stanza, leapt back down
into the road. She, thinking of Byron's bored, cool
manners, tried to imagine them screening any such
blaze of vitality.

Orestes: Do you know that I was 12 when I smelled
my first rose? That I'd never been to the country—
only to city parks? That's what I would call unnatural:

to grow up without nature, without seeing anything else grow. The children I knew never played.

Dora: What did you do?

O.: We fought. I'm playing now, at last.

Her eyes stung. She put her arm through his.

~~He on his side~~ And among the flowers: a nest, a cuttlefish of thorns, the Medusa plant, writhing, 2 red, parted lips at the end of each tentacle. In its involuted, austere sensuality Orestes saw himself.

And she—she looks out for his comfort; it matters to her. She seems not to expect to have her presence felt—a bouquet of basil on the tray with his tea, nothing more. If he thanks or praises her in terms that approach the gratitude in his heart, her eyes widen in a half bewildered, half deprecating look: good manners shouldn't make so much of common thoughtfulness. He is her guest, does he think she means to ignore him? She does nothing well—her cooking can't touch Maritsa's, her darning is grotesque—yet whatever she does

whatever issued from her hands gave pleasure, moved O. beyond all reason. Unlike an American woman who had never outgrown

who demanded

3.vii.61

The shadows on his face, his mouth opening & shutting. The look on Dora's face when, responding to his call from the garden below—O.'s head lifted, the 2 syllables of her name uttered as instinctively as a moo or a whinney; & this instinctiveness a key not just to his joy but to his confidence in hers—she

(shall they have been lovers after all?)

appeared at her window smiling: Here I am.

4.vii.61

A flood of letters yesterday. I wrote no more in the book. One would think *friends* understood the evils of correspondence.

Bit by bit D. & O. hear each other's lives—a page apiece?

(Dora): Memories of St Petersburg. The white nights. A needlecase of green & blue enamel. From there to London. The first Greek lesson. Her great-grandfather's stone house on the waterfront of which town in Crete? The young bluestocking (a photograph at 17, long braids, plump, glowing face bent gravely over her book—Shakespeare? Rostand? She no longer remembered). The wedding trip to Paris & Italy followed by—finding it hard to believe herself—nearly 40 years without leaving Greece. Byron. His nurses. Tasso. His neurasthenia. The war. ~~The lover.~~

Orestes: Parents—the goatherd and the merchant's daughter. The emigration to New York. Old Arthur Orson. The prison of the schoolyard. The father's illness. The Christmas he asks for a book & is given an orange. The traffic that night—lights flushing over the blistered ceiling like pages that turn & turn. The prize for an essay on what it means to be an American. Texas. Upstairs, the baby, the half brother, sleeps in the arms of a plush gnome.

Months had to elapse before the evening when O. sat bolt upright from his book, scalp prickling, & stared across at her in her chair, reading or sewing or whatever. He knew that if he were to ask her then & there, "Dora, Dora, what are we doing?" her reply would be promptly, reassuringly forthcoming, in that all but unaccented English of hers—"Why, my dear, we are getting through our lives!"

Save this for N. Y.?

(Or better, what M. & I arrived at, one black afternoon in Turin:

"What have you wanted out of this?"

"The experience. What else should one want?")

One day Orestes, returning on foot from town, found the iron gate of (Dora)'s property ajar. He closed it behind him, as he had done on leaving, & started for the house. In the alley of oleanders he met a stranger, a small strong middle-aged man, well enough dressed. They nodded civilly. An artisan, O. sup

On a proprietary impulse Orestes turned and called after him. Had he wanted anything? "Thank you, sir," the man replied. "I've been to the house on business." An artisan, O. supposed. Nevertheless, entering the library, he asked Dora who it had been. "Oh," she said, "are you back? Will you close the door?"

That man was now (she told Orestes) the manager of some olive groves on the mainland. Thirteen years ago, in 1941, when she had taken him as a lover, he had been in the Underground. He brought her the first British fliers to be fed & sheltered. The war over, they continued to meet. Tasso? If he had known, she dared say he would have understood & kept silent. Then he died. The lover did not wait a month before approaching her. He actually came to call! She was not at home to him. He wrote her a letter, two letters. "Ought I to have been touched? Why? It meant that he had learned very little of who *I* was in all those years. When he came today I received him & told him as nicely as I could that he must not come again. It's over. He had no education, but he had a heart and he understood. Tasso old & ill was one thing. Tasso dead is another."

(For something largely surmised, this has the ring of truth. It is how she will treat O. later on.)

There was a further change in Dora's position. Not only was Tasso dead but Orestes was present. He glowed, thinking of this & of her arrogance, reasoning that, as he was not her lover, she would never use it against him.

"ruthless pride"

Today is Independence Day.

5.vii.61

Byron came regularly from Athens to see his mother. Physically vain, he took for granted that a man as plain as he found Orestes could not attract her. He told them about his love affairs & the foreign films they were missing. Once, putting a hand on Orestes' arm, he said, "You really *are* my mother's friend, aren't you?" His tone hovered between ~~wistfulness~~ scorn & a bottomless self-pity. Another time, O. remarked that (Dora) had helped him with a translation he was making. Byron shot him a look of disbelief. "But you know Greek far better than she does. Greek is her third language."

This time Dora was present.

"Yes," she said, pleased, "if I am Greek at all, I am corrupt, late Greek. Or Byzantine like my namesake Theodora."

(But Dora must be called something else.)

"Let's hope the resemblance begins & ends with the name," said Byron, then laughed uproariously.

"Byron is not a true Greek," declared Orestes after that weekend. "Even I, in America, would never dream of directing an off-color remark at my mother."

On the subject of what was & was not authentically "Greek" Orestes fancied himself an expert. A few years later, to be sure, there would be a table of Americans in every taverna of every village, loftily contradicting one another as to what went on in the Greek mind. Few of them had O.'s Greek blood or command of the language to justify their pronouncements. But though he could talk to anyone, and did—often making a dozen new friends in an evening—there was a subtler language at which he could only guess. It was that of Good Society which had no meaning for him outside of books or jokes, yet whose members—like royalty or peasants—resembled each other more than they did 'Danes' or

'Bostonians' or 'Greeks'. To the degree that (Dora) had been formed by *class*, Orestes misunderstood her; what was conventional in her manner he found unique. But so was Greece unique, and at this point he surrenders himself lovingly to paradox. Dora, less than Greek by nature, can stand all the more for Greece in his imagination. Hadn't Shakespeare, after all, taken the foreign queen & made "Egypt" out of her—the mysterious, wealthy seasons of the Nile giving substance to the metaphor? It is in landscape, too, that O. finds Dora's correlative. In the clear dry air, in the illusory lightness of islands over water.

(I am right in clinging to my opening page.)

The hot water brought for shaving has cooled as usual. 6.vii.61—a beard begun.

How to keep recent impressions from intruding? I would never have written yesterday's last paragraph, so torturous & smug, had it not been for Mrs N.'s saying that Dora "had a place in society." The phrase clung & tickled; I've had to scratch it compulsively, thus breaking the skin of my story.

On the other hand: Byron having been away in Switzerland throughout my time in Greece, I've gone ahead and sketched in the kind of mother-son thing that leaps to *my* mind. Casual, only mildly neurotic. For all I know, Dora was the revered Mediterranean mother & B. fiercely resented Orson's intrusion (seat at head of table, tone taken with servants). It's a challenge to show something more complex & interesting than either of these banal possibilities. But what?

As Orestes grew older his imagination became an ever stronger magnetic field. New experiences whizzed past his eyes to glue themselves against the cold pull of what he had already felt.

A novel. Not a fantasia.

I should have made some sort of scheme to refer to. This is my 1st *long* piece of work, & the problems it raises are new & different from those of short stories (the single mood or action). Yet I keep imagining, wrongly perhaps, that, once I arrive at the right 'tone', the rest will follow. (My plot is of the simplest. The friendship, the marriage, the separation, basta. If the brother would only stop rearing his ugly head—)

In form & tone the book must derive from the conventional International Novel of the last century—full of scenery and scenes illustrating the at times comic failure of American & European manners to adjust to one another. Nothing of *Phèdre* here.

What could I have meant on p. 18? What would my story be concealing? I'd been toying with having Sandy *not* be O.'s brother—was that it? What "horrible action" is implied by the fact of kinship? Well, they have quarreled, Sandy doesn't feel warmly toward Orestes. Splendid! Haven't I only to remember the master's lesson, & dramatize the quarrel, the coldness? Anything rather than let it be glimpsed cutting fishily through the shimmer of a phrase.

Besides, in reading, isn't one most moved by precisely this refreshment of familiar relationships? The word 'grandmother', thanks to Proust, will have wind in its sails for the rest of time. Why shrink from doing my best for 'brother'?—or half my best for 'half-brother'!

Speaking of grandmothers, what irritates me most in what I read (& write) is the whole claptrap of presumed experience. P. C.'s new book, forwarded here, describes itself as "based on his grandmother's early life in Kentucky." It is full of *her* sensations, moral beauty, prowess in the saddle, & I don't believe a word of it. Premise & method both seem false. As if one could still see to write by the dead, pocked moon of *Madame Bovary*.

Always those "he"s and "she"s scattered about like intimate pieces of clothing, when one wants nothing so much as "I"—the anonymous nudity.

Wait—

From the moment of my arrival, I
   the world was transfigured for me. The language, the landscape, alike overwhelmed
      both of which I had pondered, as it were, in reproduction, now overwhelmed me with their (truth) and (beauty). I was more at home than I could ever have dreamed. Like a statue
         As if in a museum some figure streaked & pocked, a "Roman copy of a lost Greek original," and looked

at for decades by none but anatomy students, had suddenly been discovered to *be* the original, ~~Orestes~~ I

thanks, say, to little more than a ray of sun entering the honey-cells of marble, I felt my whole person
cleansed and restored. My skin turned olive brown.
The Latinate vocabulary to which I leaned when
thinking or speaking in English gave way to authentic,
simple forms: rock, sea, sun, wine, goat, sky.
That The land was poor & stony, that the modern
language had been, like the wine, thinned and impreg-
nated with resin, made no difference. I myself felt
poor & pungent enough to take my place among the
marble rubble, the lizards, spiny plants, clouds of dust
and sparkle of salt water—all those things on which the
Greek sun dotes & which are intolerable without it.

"Artemis is charming," I was able to write a month
later. "She is 1/3 salesgirl, 1/3 student, 1/3 Bacchante.
Through her I am learning to know this city seen here-
tofore only in dreams. We walk the night streets, drink
in the tavernas. She recites Sophocles, I reply with
Keats & Yeats. Her parents were starved to death by
the Germans. I am not in love with her, nor she with
me, though we have slept together 3 or 4 times out of
tenderness. How rarely one encounters this kind of understanding in America! Now I am waiting for her at
a café in blinding sunlight. Oh Sandy, if I could send
you the pattern cast by sun through my glass of ice
water onto this page! A whole world, pure & childlike,
awaits your coming . . ."

But the islands were calling me like sirens. I

Not a tone to be kept up for very long. I guess I'm not a "craftsman."

George plays soccer. His team won an island championship last year. (All or any of this may be wrong. Either he cannot spell or my pocket dictionary omits most of the words he uses.) He showed me a photograph: himself very snazzily dressed (check shirt, tight white trousers, pointed shoes) at some awarding of trophies; he is kissing the King's hand with a total fervor that has made the bystanding functionaries break into smiles.

"Kyrios Yannis," I conveyed, pointing to the Enfant Chic's shop, "has—a—photograph—of—me."

George repeated 3 syllables, nodding vigorously.

Blankness on my side.

But it only turned out to mean that he has seen the photograph. Chryssoula happened by in time to clear up that much, then went her way, nose in air—George's monde is not hers. He gazed after her with eyes erotically narrowed, little guessing that her eyes are for me alone.

I am a bad diarist not to have recorded this galloping passion I've inspired. The evening of my arrival I gave C. an immense bag of laundry all unwashed since Venice—shirts, pants, towels, in whose moist depths a half-full can of Nescafé had come open to encrust each item, ineradicably I'd have thought, with foul, sticky blackness. *The very next morning* there it lay, heaped, clean, in a basket hauled upstairs by two of her children.

She must have worked all night. I asked what I owed her. A shrug. What you like. I held out 100 drachmas, keeping another 50 ready in my pocket in case she spat at it. Spat! She thrust it back into my hand. It was too much—far too much! I said these were the prices of Athens (where I'm sure double or triple would be charged). Well, she took the 100, & from that day on has stalked me with the love-juice in her eye. She is past 30 but very handsome, profile of a medal, skin white & firm, spit curls, a strong heavy body (those 6 children). She makes 50 dr. a 12-hour day at the hotel. Her husband is hospitalized in Corinth (T.B.) and sends her nothing. She no longer loves him. She loves *me*!

No day begins without its bouquet of basil or bougainvillea or both, picked by her & brought to my bedside, most often by Theodoros the blondish 9 year old. Chryssoula herself follows with tea & biscuits, per-haps a bunch of grapes abstracted from another client's room. If I haven't managed to get up, she will sit on my bed, smile, gaze, stroke my face, her hands scented by another client's perfume. "Bello, come un angelo, come il Cristo." She has teased, pouted, snarled, wept, blasphemed. The whole Mediterranean repertoire. I am training her slowly to respect my privacy. It is half a joke, of course, yet I catch myself, as now, shaking not quite with laughter as I imagine a life of marriage to Chryssoula (Father & Orson have Greek wives, why not I?) or at least the scene in the Houston airport when, stepping from the plane with her & the 6 children & the black cat, I introduce them as the greatest thing since Instant Coffee: my \*N\*E\*W\* Immediate Family—just add water & serve!

7.vii.61

Let it be the following spring, the morning after Sandy arrives in Athens. (Artemis, real as you were, hail & farewell.) The brothers will be going to the Acropolis. (O. has taken Sandy there the night before, but too late, whistles were blowing, gates were shutting.) Orestes has come down to breakfast first.

(p. 11) He was a spare, nimble man, etc. . . . at his best when talking

—so long as he didn't smile: it became a grimace, one waited for him to stop. Luckily he would soon be able to resume a conversation with his brother. They were meeting now for the first time in several years.

When O. left the room, Sandy was still in bed. He was taller than his brother, also paler, younger, too young (he was 20) to be plausibly described. ~~He had never been out of America before, and, now that he had obtained permission & a basic allowance from his father to "bum around the world" for a year, he was not to go back there for more than short visits in the 7 years to come. These years would pass as in a dream. A trip would lead to an illness, an illness to a love affair, an affair to a job, a job to another trip. Beyond a certain air of passivity & idealism, there was, that morning in Athens, no trace of the traveler Sandy would become, who avoided whatever countries he knew the language of, or whose art & landscape belonged to his own cul-~~

~~tural heritage, preferring rather the relentlessly pic-~~
~~turesque, twang of bouzoukia, jabber of fisherfolk~~ His
head lay brown-haired & soft-skinned against the pillow. His eyes were almost certainly blue. He had on
white & yellow seersucker pyjamas. Orestes had
squatted by him, tousling his hair, laughing in delight,
"Come on, boy! Wake up! You're in Greece!" Then,
guessing that Sandy was too shy to dress in front of
him, he had said he would wait at the café below their
hotel, and departed, more than ever pleased with his
brother.

They were born 15 years apart, of different fathers,
& into different worlds. One father was Greek, an
immigrant; the other, an American ~~oil~~ cattleman.

The older child, born on an island off Asia Minor,
christened (Yannis), renamed first (Orson) for a bene-
factor of his father's, and only later, by himself, Orestes
—this older child had been brought as a baby to New
York, to the streets, to the prison of the schoolyard, to
2 1/2 rooms so shabby & dark that, even when he re-
visited them in the glory of adulthood, their belated

(in their glory, too, that single tenement out of the
block having escaped demolition) their belated, hard-
earned glamor filled him with ~~self-hatred~~ despair.

The younger brother (John), or Sandy to dis-
tinguish him from his father, was born in Texas, grew
up thoughtlessly in comfort and ~~love~~ love.

O. used to complain that he had no memory, &
praise me for remembering so much. He meant that I

remembered his life, his versions of things, ideas & tastes ("Did I say that? Really? You amaze me!") which had often ended by impressing me more deeply than they had ever done him. For instance, the theory (Freud's? but first expounded to me by O.) of the Mother- or Father-Substitute struck me like lightning. In New York Orson couldn't remember our ever having talked of it, yet I see it as coloring my entire

(Mrs N.: "The age at which whoever one meets makes an impression.")

I can no more unlearn what O. taught me than I can turn back the clock or regain the body I had 7 years ago. How to describe the change? I use my body less. If I swim at all, it is closer to the shore. Now that I know what liquor does to my liver, I drink ~~less~~ more. I don't take people as seriously. I move from place to place. I no longer think of myself as having a home. (Orson: Home is where the mind is.) I read more (alas) & (alas again) I *write*.

This notebook is one of 30 filled since that morning in Athens when O. made me a present of the 1st one. The stationery store had disappeared last month. But I found a shop very much like it; a girl very much like the 1st girl, pale, darkeyed, wearing the same black smock, waited on me. The sale went off easily—in Athens one can buy any drug without prescription—& I carried my current notebook out into the sun.

Orestes: What, you don't keep a journal! You amaze me!

Sandy: Oh? Why?

Orestes: Every sensitive young man keeps a record of what he does & feels, writes poems, tears them up, writes others. Didn't you know that?

Sandy: I guess so. But nothing's happened to me yet.

O.: How can you tell, if you don't know what you're like inside?

S.: Anyhow, I wouldn't call myself sensitive. That's a fightin' word in Texas.

O.: It's too early to fight with me. One day you will. I know you better than you think.

S.: You certainly imagine me better than I am.

This last is too true to have been said. If I was bewitched by Orson I see now that he was even more bewitched by me. And say so without vanity. Perhaps we all know our virtues too well to value them, but I see scant evidence, in either past or present, of the marvelous ones he assigned to me (like homework, really).

Perhaps he was in love with me—he said he found me beautiful in every way. For all I know he was (is) queer, but if so, then only on a level at which pederast & pedagogue merge into one dignified eminence. He loved anyone who was willing to learn from him. Instead of making a pass and teaching my body something new (it had mastered little but a few active verbs, all quite regular) he taught me that the mind, that *my* mind, was a holy & frightening thing. Who wouldn't have believed him? I know who. The person I am today.

As soon as he knew when to expect Sandy Orestes accepted an open invitation to lecture in Athens. It mattered hugely that his brother see "what was best" in him. "You mean there's a worst, too?" It had taken some seconds to chortle out this riposte, his first clumsy step in O.'s conversational footprints.

The lecture was delivered at the British Council, a spacious, sallow, turn of the century building, which as I write they are making plans to tear down. Audience: expatriate gentility in beads; young Greek writers & their girlfriends, unsure of their English and ashamed of their un-Bohemian manners; the great poet S—; a movie actress; a sprinkling of Americans, bearded, tongue-tied—premature beatniks. Each after his fashion worshipped O.

Title: "The Tragic Dualism of Man." Today even the speaker would be unable to reproduce this extraordinary piece of rhetoric. As on a stage backed by the unrelieved black velvet of Bertrand Russell's thought & flooded by the rainbow lights of Orestes' own euphoria, his instances leapt forth clad in their classic leotards. Body & Soul, Eros & Death, Time & Eternity, the Mayfly & the Abyss. Beethoven's gaiety, his gloom, his final ambiguous affirmation. Came also Hamlet & Horatio, Dante & Beatrice, Sancho & the Don. Mann, Joyce, Sartre, Dylan Thomas. Rembrandt & Guernica. Sandy who, for all O.'s view of him as virgin soil, had heard many of these names, had never until that evening seen anyone intoxicated by them. Orestes was. What was more, he communicated his intoxication. By the evening's end—a chorus from *The Bacchae* first in Greek, then in O.'s translation—the young faces in his audience were trembling, flashing masks of insight & purpose. And the old timers, too, had an air of agreeing that, yes, when the smoke cleared, there remained 1 or 2 arguments against total extinction of the species.

Afterwards, breathing heavily like a dancer, Orestes received their homage. He kept Sandy by his side. To those who were personal friends, perhaps 1/3 of the crowd, he said merely, "This is Sandy, he arrived yesterday," for them to exclaim with interest &, odd though it seemed, a kind of deference: here was the brother, so long awaited by their hero.

In retrospect, through the flattery, S.'s first sense of constriction.

Orestes' ideas.

If he believed in Earth (the life of sensation & toil) it was as others believed in Heaven or in going to church; it looked well, gave weight & dignity to a person.

Or: O. believed in his body as others did in their souls. His physical movements had the self-conscious grace of a martyr by Botticelli.

~~masochistic grace, inviting harm~~

Or: It was seemly (O. might have said) to taste & praise the joys of the flesh, to be Man at his most sensual. In this spirit he enjoyed both the olive & his idea of it. (From its oil came the light Plato wrote by.) He became surprisingly good at the popular Greek dances, skipping & dipping with zestful diffidence. He did not perspire like those dancers for whom the dance had been, more than play, a meditation the body itself thinking, choosing, rejoicing.

At his worktable he sits & writes. He is in heaven, it is the Platonic table he bends over, the one posited by all the cramped, gouged, unstable surfaces of his growing-up. What is he writing? No epic, not his own work, his *real* work: a mere book-review. When he has called his task "cleaning the stables" he feels better about it.

O. valued the creative act too highly to perform it.

He has told (Dora) & tells Sandy: It is my despair to have grown up without a language.

He had a hollow, radio-announcer's voice, no sooner acquired than regretted, no sooner regretted than complicated by a slanginess remembered from the streets, which made his listeners wince. Yet people were swayed by him. This intermittent wrongness of tone heightened their sense of him as mouthpiece for something mysteriously *right*. An oracle.

("Americans are struggling to express themselves in a language they scarcely know."—an English novelist.)

Sandy's ideas:
(Blank minutes follow. I study the wall. Help! Then, God be praised, Chryssoula saves me. Yesterday I was brusque with her, today I gave her a full 1/2 hour. By its end she was sitting on my lap alternately deplor-

ing my rough cheek—Why? Perchè una barba? È
brutta!—and passing candies sucked pale from her
mouth into mine. My legs are still numb. I have had to
invent a fiancée in America, to whom I am being true,
lest I wake one day to find C. toute entière beside me.)

What Sandy hasn't known is how much he means
to Orestes, & always has meant. O.: "This is what I
most regret about being so much older. Missing you,
missing your childhood." (S. is discovering that childhood has a peculiar attraction for literary people.) O.:
"But who can say? Now may be the right moment after
all. Let me look at you. What a guy!"—breaking into
the laughter of one puzzled by his luck.

Sandy responds—how can he help it? That they
are brothers means they *have* to love each other—what
else are brothers meant to do? He overlooks a slight dis-
comfort, a slight constriction of guilt that comes, he
feels, from not having prepared a place in his heart
worthy of this foreknown companion. Out of good will,
in a twinkling, the niche is made and, as it were, predated.

Avoid a 'pattern' where S. is concerned—his re-
jecting the love & trust of others. Let him remain gentle,
full of sympathy, as if he & his author were quite different people. Aren't they? Would *he* have failed Orestes
(or Lucine, or even Chryssoula)? Would he have loved
Marianne who for all her charm & experience wanted
only

Throughout these days O. and S. are abnormally

open to each other. 1st words & gestures of magic
figures shaped in darkness, or during a long spell of
fasting.

~~Eleni~~ Houston was the single topic Orestes had
resolved they would not discuss. "It is not for me to
interfere with your feelings about home."
He let Sandy feel, however, that an inner necessity,
quite divorced from whatever had gone on in his step-
father's house, had driven him forth into the world.
(Use table-talk, pp. 29-30.)
On state occasions, when the golden cloud
when dressed in the golden cloth of what he de-
sired to be, Orestes could believe that an inner necessity, quite divorced . . . into the world. True, he & his
step-father were not close. ~~Nevertheless~~ He reminded
his mother of 1000 sorrows & deprivations. And she
him. During crucial years she had bent all her energies
upon Americanizing herself, a process he came to
scorn after it had borne fruits. Both he & Sandy were
used to seeing her impulsively kissed, held at arm's
length and declared, by a red-, white- or blue-haired
neighbor, "just like one of us, Helen, angel, that's what
you are, you cute thing!" The point is that Orestes had
*not* broken with Houston. He wrote letters, sent gifts,
went home a number of years for Xmas; had been the
1st to speak the names of Homer & Shakespeare in little
Sandy's hearing. Yet it seemed always that somebody
else was doing these things, while he, Orestes, stayed
aloof in self-imposed exile. The larger-than-life Orestes

| | |
|---|---|
| Perseus | acted not from 20 trivial motives, like |
| Oedipus | press of work or shortage of money, |
| Odysseus | but from one profound one. Why had |
| Joseph (Mann) | he left home, did Sandy wonder? |
| Hamlet | Why else but that the scripture might |
| Don Q. | be fulfilled—scripture in O.'s case |
| Shelley | being the deeds of a composite liter- |
| Houdini | ary hero (beginning with Agamem- |

non's son & visiting like a pollen-
gathering bee Perseus, Oedipus, etc.) whose predica-
ment in varying forms & at varying levels of consciousness filled many an avant-garde volume read by the

Characteristics of cloth-of-gold: Ugly seams. The
wearer's skin suffers.

O. wore myth day & night like an unbecoming
color.

"I am Orestes, Perseus, Hamlet, Faust." And, in
the piping whisper of a child, unheard by him: "I am
Pinocchio."

Ah, but it made him so happy, made the ills that
befell him bearable. ~~Myth~~ Metaphor formed like ice
between him & the world. Backwards, forwards, sideways, he glided, spiraling, curvetting . . . The leaves
close in as we retreat. Their colors—reds, yellows, a
mottled purple—are those of fats & vital organs.

My God, it is sunset—where did the day go?

~~My~~ dear Mrs N.,
  ~~How can I ever thank you and Mr N. for tell you &~~
~~Mr N. what a good a delightful Mr N. what a really~~
~~enjoyable~~ How can I possibly thank

Dear~~est~~ Lucine,
  A few lines to ~~say I am thinking about you. Are~~
~~you all right? I wish so much~~ wonder if you are still
afloat, & where. Part of me wishes very much ~~it~~ I had
sailed away with you. ~~Do you think you will ever come~~
~~back?~~ Will this reach you in Athens? What is it like in
summer? (You needn't tell me; I know.) Here nothing
changes appreciably. A drizzle of Danes has descended.
Giorgios caught an immense frowning Fish which
everybody was invited to share. He wants to be remembered. So does the Enfant Sick. I guess I'm at work. ~~Am~~
~~I remembered?~~ Please send me a card.

Well, those are written, plus one to Houston,
sealed in last night's bottles & flung into the foaming
tide. A whole day (8.vii.61) frittered away. I still feel
quite awful, capable, even, of returning by fall, as
promised in my letter home.
  Those gallons of wine! George! Those girls—I
never want to see *any* of them again. Least of all a voluble
Sunflower named Inge who must already have taken 3
of the Enfant's boys into the pine trees when her whim
shifted to the New World. And into me as well she sank
her golden teeth. There are marks.
  In writing the N.'s I felt stupid & awkward, as if
I had wronged *them*, her deputy parents, rather than L.

What I want now is to sketch in the scene of the lemon groves, the panegyri, & make it express a number of things. Among them:

1) The community. The abbot. The light. Music & smells.

2) The rapport between Sandy &

3)

But not today.

9.vii.61
Or today.

This noon, leaving Inge & her friends waiting for the boat to Hydra, I did at least take the 10 minute ferry trip to the mainland & walked the mile or so out to the lemon groves. None of it familiar. Had hoped to find the clearing, the tall (pepper?) trees under which the musicians played, the stones where the fires & spits had been. Not a trace, as after a fairy feast, not even gossamer or the ring of mushrooms. Narrow earthen paths, rows of trees stretching deep on either side. Blink of perspectives—near, far, near, far—in green, dry heat as I passed.

10.vii.61
The morning of the panegyri found them bathing in the cove below Orestes' cottage.

It was in a remoter cove that O., swimming one day, had discovered, wedged among rocks, a water-worn, barnacled fragment of statuary: the upper head (brow, eye, curling locks) of a marble youth. He treasured it above all his belongings. From then on, when he swam, magic upheld him. An element in which anything was possible.

(Dora), O., Sandy, Maritsa and the baby. A palmetto sunshade had been put up. They advise Sandy to use it, but he is plunging in & out of the water, charging here & there with the dog. The brown sand is flecked with tar; soon his feet are black. He sees for the 1st time the beautiful 'skeleton' of a sea-urchin, its crust of green- or rose-tinted bisque, stippled, as in formal 18th century stucco, with dotted radii diminishing in size toward a little empty place at the crest.

"Yes, but those are dead stars," said Orestes. "Look out there! Deep in their cool, luminous heaven live the real ones, revising slow, black, threatening constellations."

"What are you saying, Kyrie Oreste?" cried Maritsa, and, when he had translated it for her: "Ah! Imagine!"

"Watch out for them," said (Dora). She removed her bathing-slipper & exhibited a cluster of minute black points sealed beneath the thickened skin of her heel. "Those are from just after the war."

Sandy reached into the shade to touch the place, wonderingly. Their bodies, Dora's and Orestes', fascinated him in ways he hardly knew how to think about.

Seen objectively, Maritsa was shapelier, more sexual, her contours firm & sweet as the melon she now sliced for them. Sandy himself had fine metallic

hairs on his arms and legs, he turned a lean white belly
to the sun. But what was this? Mere youth. It didn't
give out the exotic air sense of alienation between spirit
& matter

the romance of accomplished individuality which
reached him from (Dora) & his brother.

Orestes' thin body lay, propped on elbows, knees
bent; a locust carved out of oiled walnut. His ungoggled
eyes gave back the horizon. What must have happened
*inside* him to cause that one white hair among the others
sprouting round his nipple? The sunken places above
his collarbones, the waxlike glimmer of his shins. Dora
—the scant fat forming in pearls, thoughtlessly, between arm & breast, the urchin spines in her foot—a
constellation in negative; a destiny no longer in the
heavens, waiting, but *incorporated*, part of her. Her thighs
were shelled with flesh an ivory browned more by age
than by sun. These bodies woke no desire in Sandy, yet
his imagination ran riot through scenes in which they
must have participated—separately of course!—in
order to achieve

yet he yearned to a degree that shocked him, to
possess their memories of action & delight, so deeply
incorporated now in those 2 forms rising from the sea,
streaming with brilliant drops that paled to salt in the
day's dry blaze.

(The sea of the Past. Lot's wife?)

The baby was still 3/4 spirit. It flickered fatly,
sweetly, a fire in their midst. Orestes would not tire of
playing with it, taking it back into the water on his

shoulders. A look on (Dora)'s face struck Sandy. Was it possible that, 20 years older than O., she saw in him— whose attempts at play impress S. as so much nostalgic artifice—reserves of innocent animality?

(Sharpen & reinforce this attraction she feels. The showdown is only hours away.)

A revery without end: If X. were young, if I were old. If I were young, if Y. . . .

They had stopped warning Sandy. He lay in the sun & burned.

The Panegyri.

They set out in mid-afternoon. Only Kanella remained behind, tail hopefully wagging even as they glided forth from the dock. A sheer whitish blue rippled on the water like silk. Kosta steered. Maritsa & Orestes, holding a child apiece, sang songs. From the stern, beaming like royalty, Dora & Sandy watched the gold-green shore approach.

When they landed, "We'll start ahead," said (Dora), taking Sandy's arm. They followed a narrow earthen path.

These two were gay & easy together, pleased with each other's (reality) which O.'s advance descriptions had done little to prepare them for. He still knew best, of course, knew them—didn't he?—better than they would ever know themselves or one another. Their friendship was but some slight retrograde expertise in the wider heavens of Orestes' life, from which they were to ~~guide shine down on~~ return his light.

(And time will prove him right. When O. no longer gives it meaning, their intimacy fades.)

At the festival. Continuous music, warm gusts of rosemary & fat, lambs on spits, sun-shafts turning the blue smoke to marble. It would last hours and was paced accordingly. "What we must first do," said Dora when the others had caught up, "is to pay our respects to the abbot."

This person stood black and bearded in the shade of the largest pepper tree. He offered Sandy a strong, white, soiled hand & fixed him with professionally piercing eyes, speaking all the while.

Orestes (translating): He welcomes you to Greece & wants to know your age. He won't believe you're 20, you look 16, kid. I'll tell him 18. They thought I was 25 until I grew a moustache. Ha ha!"

(Somewhere else: "Ha ha!" exclaimed O. on a rising inflection, the notes exactly a fourth apart, as at the end of Manon's Gavotte.)

Tiny glasses of ouzo were served, followed by tumblers of cold water & rose-flavored jam on spoons. The entire clearing, trees, glimpses of hills and sea, took on the air of an interior (frescos, mirrors) where, in the absence of the saint whose Day it was, a man in long black robes had agreed to play host.

After further civilities the guests were released.

O. (as they moved away): He wanted to know where you were going after Greece, Sandy. I told him, back to America. He would never have believed a boy your age had money & freedom to travel so extensively.

~~Sandy: Who misrepresented my age to him in the first place?~~ Sandy nodded. At that moment he couldn't imagine leaving (Diblos), let alone arriving in Cairo, Bombay, Yokohama!

A Greek shopkeeper in Houston had given him 5 lbs. of caramels wrapped in colored papers "for the children of Greece." These now, alerted by Orestes, came up in droves to claim them, stopping, however, a courteous meter from the young foreigner.

O.: They're shy. In Greece the stranger is a god. Especially if he's blond & blue-eyed. Hey, fella, (slapping Sandy on the shoulder) you're turning rosy, too!

Each child waited gravely for his sweets &, on receiving them, broke into a slow smile.

O.: That's the smile of the kouros, the archaic smile. Pose a Greek child for a snapshot, his shoulders lift like wings, his arms stiffen at his side, and he smiles. How full of pride that smile is! It's the 1st photograph of Man taken by his new young god—before they've learned how to torment one another.

"What are you saying?" a little boy must have asked. He listened soberly to whatever O. replied. A last phrase sent them all laughing & scrambling away.

Orestes: Greek children love me because I treat them like adults.

Their fathers, meanwhile, had sent many cans of wine to the table cleared for (Dora)'s party. It was the work of the next hour to consume these, toasting the givers or whoever happened by. To eat: a cube of cheese, crust of bread, 2 olives, a segment of grilled octopus. Small plates piled up empty. They could be used later, said O., to throw at Kosta's feet, if he danced well. Kosta blushed.

They had all danced, Sandy included—connected by handkerchiefs to Maritsa & Dora, to numberless others forming a great swaying crescent. Then this simple dance would end, another kind of tune begin, a single young fisherman spin, dip, snap, leap his way through it, eyes always on the earth; or an older dancer, closer to earth in another sense, allude

execute slow allusions to the passion & agility he no longer commanded.

Presently Sandy was able to watch with—and Dora without—astonishment his brother & Kosta alone in the dancing place. ~~Circling one another~~ H~~h~~issing like serpents, Kosta wriggling his powerful shoulders rapidly, seductively in parody of a belly-dancer (fat, clown-white, a dream of beauty to any man present), they circled one another until, suddenly, on an emphatic beat

The very hissing is sexual—sssss! It's of course the consonant missing from a married woman's name (put in the genitive: Mr Pappas, Mrs Pappa, etc.) and so commends itself to the dancer as a tiny linguistic feature related to moustache & phallus, one more fine feather of virility—

beat, Kosta jumped & landed not on the ground but in midair, with legs wrapped about O.'s waist, head fallen back, shoulders still undulating. The two pairs of arms outstretched, the 2 moustached heads oppositely inclined—something was there of Narcissus & his image, something of the Jack of Clubs. Then they sprang apart, to revolve separately, barely smiling, until the piece ended.

"Come now," said Orestes to his brother, later, after a fresh can of wine had been drunk. "You and I this time."

The state of high spirits known as kéfi had descended upon their table. (Dora) at whom Sandy had looked questioningly, merely laughed & said, "Of course!"

Already the instruments were wrangling happily together. Sandy contented himself with repeating, most gracefully, he thought, the basic steps Orestes indicated—forward, sideways, snap your fingers—while the latter went on to dip, whirl, touch earth, strike shoe with palm, resoundingly, rise, dip again, & abruptly, facing Sandy, whisper *Now*.

"I'm too heavy, I'll knock you over."

"Don't worry, come on, boy!"

He places his hands on O.'s shoulders. "Hup!" cries Orestes, and S., with a last desparing look at the world, springs upwards & backwards to lock his thighs around his partner's waist. The rest of him has fallen free, head inches from the ground, arms trailing. Upside-down, trees, tables, (Dora), the colored wool embroidery of her bag, everything exuberantly revolves. O.'s face grins down: the look of the initiator. Now Sandy remembers to snap his fingers. O. hisses lightly, provocatively. It ends all too soon. "Up!" cried Orestes, & their uncouplement is effected to applause. S. lurches backwards, sustained by the music's beat, by nothing else. His dizziness has hardly passed before O. confronts him—"Ready? Now brace yourself. Hup!"—and in a flash the whole staggering weight of another body has become *his*. But he's mad, S. thinks, I can't hold him up! as they go reeling towards a group of tables and Orestes, blissful & trusting, smiles up at him. I cannot! Sandy has opened his mouth to cry—the blood pounding beneath his sunburn—he cannot—yet within seconds it appears that he can; he can, he can. Power & joy fill him. His eyes fill. He can dance under his brother's weight. Then it is over, & the music, too.

"Bravo," said Dora, welcoming them back. "You're going to make an excellent Greek, Sandy."

It had earned them *lots* more wine.

An hour later (Dora) looked at Sandy more closely. "I think we shall have to take you home."

"Ah, no!" from Orestes. It was a *good* panegyri; Sandy must be allowed to see it all—look, they were carving the lamb at last!

S. (earnestly): I'm not drunk, you know.

Dora: No, but you are bright red. Look at him, Orestes, he's badly burned.

O.: Ah, it's too bad, etc. The upshot (to be written?) is that Kosta takes his family, Dora & Sandy back to the House, then returns to bring Orestes home when the panegyri has run its course.

Sandy feels nothing, notices nothing. The wine has

numbed him. He is put to bed.

(Make the dancing less euphoric?)

Just before dawn something woke him. The gray light barely tinged his sheets. Burning all over, head throbbing, Sandy got up to peer into the front room. Orestes' bed had not been slept in. Nor was he to be found lying face-down among the cactuses outside his door. No one was anywhere. Had there been a sound? a voice? It came to S. that if he were to walk down those steps, under those eucalyptuses at every moment more visible, & reach that last tree at its point parallel to the façade of the House, he would see—What? He hardly knows; he would simply *see*.

He walks there. He does see.

First he has met, on his way, Kosta in great good humor, making for his quarters—"Ah, Kyrie Sandy," and touches the sunburn inquiringly, laughing, nodding.

Then the dog Kanella, tail not wagging, puzzled at the edge of the terrace.

20 yards distant stands Orestes. He has been out all night. Sober as stone, he is nonetheless hesitant, blinking, off guard, as if having just gained this level & found it unfamiliar. Between him & the House (Dora) has appeared, in her nightgown and dark blue flannel robe. At the sight of it, Sandy's teeth begin to chatter. Neither sees *him*. Her feet are bare, her hair unkempt. O. breaks the silence, but in Greek.

"The servants," she whispers, warning him.

The air grows a shade paler. It dawns on the audience that she has had no sleep. Her whole body shakes once. She asks where Orestes has been.

He replies. It sounds harmless, plausible. A night of drink, of talk—anything. A few hours sleep at ——'s house. *Kosta* hadn't felt like leaving.

"My dear," she said with a light, hysterical laugh. "You're lying to me. Don't."

A very long pause. She turned her clenched face from him, savagely.

"Dora, I never dreamed," said Orestes.

"Nor I," she sobbed. "Help me. Oh my friend. It came too suddenly. I couldn't control. Do you understand. It's not what I."

He goes to her now, draws her hands down from her face, saying her name. She stares: half panic, half outrage. "Go to bed, Orestes."

He will not. She has asked for his help.

~~She throws herself into his arms.~~

~~She gave him a look from which reasonableness had been scrupulously withdrawn and threw herself~~

"Go, go," she sighed. "I'm all right. Go to bed."

Sandy, from behind his tree, obeyed her. Back to the cottage he sped, unseen, bone-cold, with clacking teeth.

In 5 minutes he hears O. come in, say his name &, when he doesn't answer, fall on the bed in the front room.

The day was brighter when Orestes spoke again. "Are you awake, Sandy? Do you feel better? Shall I fetch you a glass of water?"

Now S. lets O. tell what has happened. Orestes is, as usual "amazed", "profoundly disturbed", wonders if he will be able to "cope" with (Dora)—it will be for *him*, naturally, to take charge of the situation.

"Shall I pretend it never happened? Or try to help Dora accept & overcome her feelings?"

Orestes often borrowed this rhetorical device from Greek tragedy. Never "How did you come here?" but "Did you walk today? or take your bicycle?" So that to answer him (unless one can say *I swam* or *I flew*) one must admit that he has foreseen, in his wisdom, every alternative.

The alternative here—the unforeseen one—would be to return the love.

(Dora's more 'Byzantine' device: "I suppose, in this heat, you came by boat . . . ?")

Anyhow, he talks & talks. The prison of words. S. may fall back to sleep in the midst of it—as I am about to do, myself, this hot, hot afternoon.

It *is* a crucial scene. How it was actually resolved I must try to remember. ~~From then on~~

Outdoors, alone.

The setting sun. A clear golden

From the horizon a golden-pink light flows. When I lower my eyes it is to see water breaking on a rock a yard or two below my bare feet. The waves are small, their bravura limitless. One could name

(Sandy, feverish) tried to name their different

movements: the ~~swirl~~ pirouette, the recoil, the beat missed on purpose, the upward hurl of white nets, the

pounce, the pause for reflection; but Use this to      no two were ever accomplished with complement   quite the same motive or, for that mat- description on  ter, success. Again & again an ornate p. 17        sequence would inexplicably break

down; the sea would shrug, collapse, retire into a slot, a coulisse prudently hollowed out of rock beforehand. For an instant the stage would be empty; one felt a sad kinship with the effaced gesture. Then a new star

a crash of harps! A new, staggeringly assured star, all mist & fretted crystal, had leapt and 'frozen'—like only the greatest dancers, a second longer than anyone would have thought possible, in the tense, vivid air.

His feet alone gave scale to the spectacle. He tried to keep them in sight.

The play of water: a fou rire that goes on & on. Successions of rapid, fluid shocks, unending variations, each as simple, each as elaborate, as the last. It bears no message.

It wrote a message in invisible ink, not to be read for 1000's of years, upon the worn, slotted surface of the rock.


12.vii.61

He felt (Dora)'s hand on his forehead. "I came out to see how you were. You looked feverish at lunch."

She sat down beside him. He gazed avidly into her

face for signs of ~~unhappiness~~ her own fever. None showed.

"Kosta is bringing some bismuth from town. If you're no better tomorrow we'll have the doctor."

"I'll be all right. I'm all right now," said Sandy. It was what he said & said during the fortnight that followed. There were days, furthermore, when D. & O., occupied by their own dilemma, gave every appearance of believing him. They never told him to stay in bed. He was free to wander about, thinner & weaker daily, as if he were not a child. The doctor materialized. When the bottle of medicine had been emptied, no one suggested that it be refilled. Sandy would rise from lunch, having eaten some soup & 2 spoonfuls of Dora's cornstarch confection which reappeared, larger & sturdier it seemed, from meal to meal. He would totter down to the water's edge with his book & his blanket, there to remain until one of them came for him.

Orestes, he supposed, kept him informed of the unfolding drama. What (Dora) had said, what he in turn had replied. Somehow, by the time Sandy left the hospital—they have stayed on in Athens to be near him —it was all resolved. Her great wave of feeling had spent itself.

Psychologically (O. explains) it was to have been expected. A final sexual upsurge that had little to do with him personally. As he, rather than another, happened to be her guest, he had borne the brunt of it. Patiently, reasonably, he now faced with her all the contributing motives—the delayed shock of widowhood, the sense that this had not brought Byron closer to her. She ended by seeming to accept his interpretations gratefully. She would keep Orestes as her dearest friend.

(In fact she is going to America with him.)

"You see," said O. gravely, "Dora means too much to me now, for me to risk the ambiguities, the tensions of a sexual relationship. She sees it, she agrees with me. We're more than ever in perfect accord, having lived through those anxious weeks together."

Something of the sort, put into talk or not, gets through to Sandy. In his mind Orestes & Dora perform a final somersault: they have chosen imagination, withstood the coarse quicksand of the senses. Platonic love! S. lies back on his pillow, impressed.

(Dora, 5 years later, in her narrow N. Y. flat, studying Chinese. She has aged, seems paler & softer, from spending less time out of doors, perhaps. Her brush, her inkstone. "This is the ideogram of power, this of language, this of island." She & Sandy spend a sweet, elegiac hour together; he is going abroad, who knows if they will meet again? Is he going to Greece? She would like to give him some letters. Speaking of Orestes, as of a character in a novel, she says, "He was Greek, yes, but with the glaze of a Turk.") (It's after hearing—from me—of this visit that O. writes his letter full of hurt withdrawal: Dora's charm had "blinded" me; I was no longer the serious, child-like, brother-loving etc. . . . It strikes me now that behind these

words lay his dismay over my not having sought to bring
him & Dora together again. "Love is not merely feeling,
but action," he wrote. A dreamer to the last.)

Wait—
One conversation he did remember, from his 1st
week in the hospital. The doctors had yet to determine
what the matter was. Orestes stuck his daily bouquet in
water & seated himself. To cheer S. up, he remarked
what a lucky guy he was to be able to afford a private
room—all O.'s experiences of hospitals had been wards
full of moaning & dying. Well, Sandy was just a gilded
youth.

S.: I still don't feel I'm really sick. It doesn't seem
possible to *be* sick in Europe.

O.: Oh? Were you often sick at home?

S.: Oh, you know—measles, colds, a sprained
ankle. I'd stay in bed and let Mother bring me soup &
orangeade.

O.: You enjoyed being sick at home, is that what
you mean?

S.: Well, I guess so—compared to *this* place. Did I
say something wrong?

O.: Wrong? Of course not. But my dear Sandy,
you understand what you *are* saying, don't you?

S. (after thinking): That I'm sick now because I
want to go home?

Delighted by his pupil, Orestes develops the theme
handsomely. Tuberculosis—the 19th cent. disease—
smog of conventions, lungs failing for lack of a purer,

fresher air. Asthma. Then comes cancer—20th cent. disease: gnawing of GUILT. Homesickness would naturally express itself by upset tummy & bowels.

Sandy (recapitulating): So I'm not really sick at all?

O.: Of course you are. I never said that.

S.: But only in my mind?

Orestes reassures him; there can be more talk. It is a subtle point, though, & he may never fully grasp it. More & more he ~~is like the oyster who can't feel the grit for the pearl~~ loses faith in phenomena uncolored by the imagination's powerful dyes.

Some days pass. Sandy turns vivid yellow to the very eyeballs, thus facilitating a diagnosis. "What did I say?" joked Orestes, after expressing concern.

"That I wasn't sick."

"No—that you were a gilded youth!"

July. Sandy leaves the hospital. His father has cabled him to fly home; out of question to proceed, as planned, to Egypt & the Orient. At first S. means to ignore it, to travel by freighter, working his way if need be. As he has known no hardship, the prospect intoxicates. Also, he has gathered from Orestes that sons must *rebel* against their fathers. O., however, is shocked. Learned doctors have prescribed rest & proper food; a diet of amoebas & ghee would be "suicidal." They compromise. Sandy will travel through Italy & France with his brother & (Dora), & sail for New York when they do. This pleases everybody.

Dora's house in Athens. Rents frozen since the war, no income from it. She worries about having money in America. She decides to sell

She decided finally to travel wrapped, as it were, like Cleopatra, in one very fine Oriental rug which, sold, would keep her for the rest of her stay. She wanted not to be a burden to Orestes.

It relieved them both that Sandy was to travel with them. While he was in the hospital, (Dora) & Orestes had begun to miss the company of a 3rd person. By themselves, their talk broke out at strange levels, painfully, as if a device to regulate pressure had been damaged. ("Dora, you went ahead and sold that mirror! Ah, that makes me very cross with you." Or: "I think I'll plan to stay on in Paris with my friends there. *You* go to N. Y.; I'm too old for the New World.")

In saying that their crisis was over, Orestes was mostly correct. Certainly it would never be repeated. But what neither took into account—fancying themselves too civilized, too enlightened—was the sediment of shame & resentment on her side, and on his a blitheness left over from having been found desirable by a woman he idolized

a blitheness that emerged as the issues receded. One never minds having been found desirable.

With this one secret of Dora's captured & tamed, O. assumed wrongly that it had no jealous mate. It did, though—a 2nd secret that circled round them both for some time, unperceived. It was that Dora disliked him.

During these last weeks in & out of Athens Orestes met the Hollywood producer: a Greek-American, like himself, sitting at the next table in a café. They fell into

(This will be a strand running throughout the book—O.'s relations with Greek intellectuals, as gleaned here & there over the years. On 1st arriving he naturally seeks them out—men of letters, painters, etc. There is great warmth on both sides. They have felt, what with the war, extremely isolated. O. sets about correcting this state of affairs. He collects their books with a view to translating them, placing stories & poems in American magazines. Before leaving Athens he persuades 2 or 3 painters to ship some of their best work to him in N. Y. where he will arrange for it to be shown. And he does what he has promised. In time there is an exhibition, the stories & poems do get published. What goes wrong? Well, the pictures don't sell; the magazines are small, ephemeral, do not pay. Shipping costs actually cause the artists to lose money. Certain British philhellenes, perhaps more out of spite than taste, have things to say about the quality of O.'s translations. None of it, really, is his fault. He has done his best. But several years will have to elapse before Greece is chic, & it will take a more persuasive figure than Orestes to make it so—Mrs Kennedy, for instance, or Melina Mercouri. In any case, he returns to find this chill on the part of men who had once clasped him to their hearts. Those who remain loyal aren't the most distinguished. With one exception. The poet & novelist V— who with his English wife found O. brilliant &

charming from the 1st, & never revise their opinion.
Voici pourquoi. Along with his immense, mystical odes,
at once symbolic and "folkloristic," V. was the author
of an historical novel, a picaresque 19th cent. version
of the *Agamemnon* in which the hero, back from a
campaign against the Turks, is murdered by his wife &
her lover, then avenged by his children. In this book,
admired by every imaginable reader, Orestes saw the
makings of an excellent film. He suggested it over coffee
to the Hollywood producer, the latter took fire, read
the novel & asked O. to do the screenplay, giving him a
contract to sign the day before he & Dora leave Greece.
Poor O.! If he had paid his usual attention to myth, he
would have known that Hollywood destroys the artist.
The process takes years: private planes, costly dinners,
conferences leading nowhere. At the end his script is discarded, but the film made. It can still be seen in Greece.
O. is left with the taste of ashes in his mouth, and V.,
left rich & famous, will not hear a word against O.)

Oh dear, I've met Byron.
I broke off & went swimming. Then, from the café,
watched the boat from Athens come in & him get off,
and thought no more of it until, looking up 20 minutes
later, there he was returning along the waterfront, with
packages, & talking to of all people the Enfant Chic.
The latter smiled venomously at me (George had joined
me on the beach, refusing to budge when the E. C.
called him) & said something to Byron out of the corner
of his mouth. B. looked, stopped, abandoned the

Enfant, came over to my table.

"I know who you are. My mother's so fond of you. I'm Byron. Will you let me give you another ouzo? I'm afraid I've been remiss about doing the honors of Diblos."

He is very handsome, very much a man. Slender, well-preserved for over 40 (just Orson's age?). Beautiful hands, knuckles & wrists, tanned, manicured. A flat gold watch, a blood-red seal-ring he removed to show me. "It's a good one, isn't it? Actually it was my mother's engagement gift to my father."

He wanted to know where I was staying, where I ate, whom I knew. An anecdote at the expense of the N.'s. But I *was* comfortable, & *liked* Diblos? Good! His relief just skirted megalomania: the island was his, it had better be run properly.

About Orson:

"How's your brother? He's in Athens, I've heard. Will he be joining you here? I see. Well, it's of no importance. He'd left some books & things on the place, but there couldn't be less rush, he can pick them up any weekend. Tell me, what's he done since that film? Published lots of things? Brilliant chap. The talks we used to have!"

I gather B. & his wife are separated. "I usually bring a girl along. The house is conveniently inconvenient. No, this weekend I'm a bachelor, brought reports to read instead. In fact I'll be off now, I've a putt-putt waiting. Look, come for a drink tomorrow—sixish? Splendid. Cheerio."

Well, Orson doesn't get his cottage, I'm afraid.

B. bubbles over with charm & good will. What a disappointment! My own (Byron) I'd seen more as the type of heavy, petulant, weak young man so often found in the wake of a powerful mother (Frau Doktor & son in Tangier). *My* Byron would greedily have examined those "books & things" of O.'s, hoping for something to use against him.

( A scene—the Enfant Chic present. The photograph is shaken out of a book. *Yes.*)

Or is the real Byron, in the last analysis, weak? For all his charm, a point keeps recurring when every woman—mistress, wife, mother—rises & tiptoes out of his life, as from the living-room of an irksome host, to tear her hair & ask the mirror in the guest john '*How* will I ever get through this evening (or marriage or whatever)?' Doesn't he feel this? And what need has he to be so British in Greece? The vogue nowadays is for Americans & Scandinavians. (This last after 2 more ouzos.)

13.vii.61

A package has come for me but no one can find it. Chryssoula is at home, unwell. The pyjama'd manager says it has gone back to the P. O. which is shut now, as of noon. And tomorrow's Sunday—Bastille Day. Seeing my face, he cries placatingly, "That's all right!"

One last scene in Athens. The Hat on the Acropolis.

(The contract is signed, they sail that evening, Orestes decides he needs a hat.)

Sandy: I thought you didn't like hats.

Dora: We're leaving the worst heat behind us.

Orestes: Won't they be wearing hats in Rome & Paris?

D.: In midsummer! Do they in New York?

O. (laughing): Don't they? They do in all the ads.

S.: Well, you're the one who lives there.

Orestes: Ah, Sandy, I've become so Greek. I think of America as a country known through ~~films~~ movies & magazines, where the sidewalks are made of gold.

They entered the shop. Orestes made his wishes known to the clerk who brought out hat after hat for him to try on. Dora & Sandy exchanged glances. A long time passed before O. said, "I think this one will be suitable."

It was an expensive 'young executive' model— gray-green felt, snap brim, ribbon, feather, the works. On hearing that it was a Borsalino, imported from Italy, & that while he waited the shop would stamp his initials in gold on the inner leather band, Orestes' joy knew no bounds.

His companions hardly knew where to begin.

Sandy: You look like a businessman.

Dora: It's not a hat for warm weather. You'll have a stroke!

S.: Is that feather real?

Dora: For summer, a straw hat—

S.: We'll be in Italy tomorrow. You can buy a Borsalino there, probably at half the price.

D.: Tasso used to wear a gondolier's hat, it was

always cool & becoming. This looks like the Greek-American dream.

But no. Orestes wanted this hat, and at once. He *was* a G.-A.; such a hat *was* his dream. "You are sophisticated," he informed them, "but I am more sophisticated than you. I choose this hat precisely because to wear it means that I've arrived."

"Arrived where?" cried his ~~friends~~ tormentors.

O. kept laughing. "It means you're rich, respected, a big shot. Do you want me to go to Hollywood bareheaded? My taste may be bad, but this isn't a question of taste. I could never have *had* this hat a month ago. Now I deserve it."

It was an odd moment. Both sides were, & were not, in agreement. The subject was dropped and never ostensibly

only to be resumed at a higher level.

Orestes wore his hat out onto the street. "Shall we walk up to the Acropolis? Will that tire you, Sandy? We ought to make a ceremony of our last day."

(No one is seeing them off. Dora has been purposely vague about this, well, elopement. From her point of view it's all to the good that Byron has been in Switzerland these past months—let his wife be ~~pregnant~~ ~~difficult~~ in a clinic, something glandular. O. has been more precise. A group of *his* friends, students, very motley, turn up at the sailing, with gifts. Disturbing Dora not at all. These young people will never have entrée to her world.)

"Everything depends," said Orestes cheerfully, "on

the spirit in which one enters the arena. It's a game."
He was speaking of Hollywood. "I can stop playing
when I choose. And I'll be left financially able to do my
real work, the work that demands my total dedication."

~~They nodded, swayed by the old refrain.~~

They paused to admire the Tower of the Winds,
then climbed a narrow street of pretty houses in dis-
repair.

"This may have vanished when we return," said
(Dora). "The Americans want to dig here."

"How terrible," said Sandy.

D.: When you think that it's Byron's Athens, after
all, this district . . .

Orestes: Byron's?

D.: The poet.

O.: Ah. Because I thought you meant *Byron.*
Dora's son, whom you haven't met, is named Byron,
Sandy.

S. nods.

O.: Well, let them dig. There may be treasures
under these old houses.

D.: But the houses are so pretty!

O.: My dear Dora, prettiness can't compare in
ultimate value with a head—with an *elbow*—by
Phidias. I don't say they'll find one, but more power to
them for looking.

(Mention his underwater fragment?)

Dora: Ah, we shall never lack for masterpieces.
We take care of them. It's prettiness we're forever
sacrificing, sweeping away.

(To be felt in the foregoing: O.'s own past is the issue. A dream of poverty & rubbish swept away to reveal the meaningful plan of temple or market underneath.)

They arrive at the Acropolis, pass through the Propylea onto the blind, bald marble hill. Orestes makes for the Parthenon. Midway he pauses. Runnels of dampness the hot wind would otherwise have dried leak from inside his new purchase.

His eyes also are moist.

He has told them before, he tells them again: his first glimpse of this building, while driving that long straight road from the Piraeus to Athens. Constantly in sight, squat at 1st, more & more elevated as they neared it, stood this Thing, golden

honeycolored, ~~fingered by light~~

a lyre the sun fingered. How dispassionately he had eyed it, not recognizing his oldest dream until, with a cry, just as it vanished from his range of vision, he fell forward onto the taxi's floor. It had been the Parthenon!

They admire it with him.

Sandy (after a bit): And that smaller building over there? I forget its name.

D. (who has draped her whole head in a chiffon scarf, Pernod-yellow, fluttering tightly like a flag): That's the Erectheum. The one *I* love.

O.: I should think that you would love it, Dora. It is a feminine building, all elegance & charm. And of course (laughing) that magnificent balcony—you know what balconies on buildings mean, according to

Freud! Even in French, am I right? la balcon has become a euphemism for female charms.

~~Sandy: And what are "female charms" a euphe-~~
~~mism for?~~

~~O.: Touché.~~

(Dora): (Something about its original use. A holy
place.)

S. (reading the Blue Guide): The Turks used it for
a harem.

Orestes: You see!


14.vii.61

What I want, here at what could be an organ-point
in the book, is this "Dialogue on the Acropolis" in
which, starting from a difference in taste (the hat),
Orestes' & Dora's two ways of being, their as it were
moral differences, are set forth. To keep, if possible, the
2 buildings as symbols.

| *Dora* | *Orestes* |
|---|---|
| Erectheum | Parthenon |
| Monet | Michelangelo |
| Rameau (Schumann) | Beethoven |
| Racine | Shakespeare |
| Herbs | Flowers |
| The Subtle | The ~~Monumental~~ Sublime |

The temples themselves:

The famous one, noble, simple (deceptively so, O.
will insist) rises in sunlight, marvelous for its bigness

its openness: a sire, a seer. The father in a novel about
a happy childhood.

The other by comparison seems dangerously complex & arbitrary

Japanese      a small-boned woman

a dressing-table at which somebody has assembled
the various elements—powder, eye-shadow, a pleated
~~robe~~ teagown—of a 'je ne sais quoi' & vanished, for no
more than a moment, surely, into another room.

Orestes: One lives for the sake of one's tragic insights.

(Dora): If that is true, one still has access to them
at one's dressing-table—more often than at one's
prie-dieu.

O. (magnanimous): Let us say that as *symbols* these
2 temples have equal power, but that the states they
symbolize do not.

~~Dora (amused): You are more human than I am,
is that it?~~

Heavens, am I going to have to *read* Hegel &
Marx?

Both buildings are badly flawed. Yet, between
them, they represent, with a purity & clarity far from
mortal,* the two modes of being. The moon, the sun;

*far from mortal—here's my mistake. My Dia-
logue pits 2 dreams against each other, instead of living
antagonists. Life, Art—they are words. It's on a lower
level that the mongoose closes with the cobra. In a
footnote. In the dust.

the earth, the soul; the wife, the god. What other site in the world so quickens & cleanses the heart? (The *blackness* of Chartres.)

The sun & moon together in the sky.

Still, after a while, prompted by the blurred clamor from below, if not by the voices of those who like one-self have climbed this high & seen fit to describe the experience to one another, it was to the parapet one went, to see what one had left behind. There, below, lay the city, smoking, sparkling. Poverty. Urgency. Cats patrolling the rooftiles, boys playing soccer, women with burdens. Men in pyjamas at 4 p.m. Further off: one's hotel, the house of a friend, the restaurant at which, months earlier, one had become involved in an ugly scene; the bank, the hat-shop; the swimming-pool; the gardens with peacock & papyrus

& the sparse fright-wigs of the papyrus round a pool on whose cement bottom a honeycomb pattern of sun will be trembling; a duck's bamboo bill

A gust of wind lifts Orestes' hat, which has been resting on the parapet, and drops it into ~~the city~~ the cactuses beneath.

He won't reclaim it. To Dora & Sandy: "The gods are on your side."

They sail that night. (A hue & cry at customs. The marble half-head found by O. is 1st confiscated then declared ~~a fake~~ worthless, & courteously returned.)

George keeps sitting with me on the beach. Now that we've shared the fly-by-night Danish beauty, he has decided we are friends. I cannot plumb the mysterious shallows of his nature. Setting out to please, he nevertheless sees no way of doing so except through his mere presence, the offer of 1 initial cigarette & subsequent acceptance of 5. As he rises to leave, a drop of soft soap: "You good man."

I had never asked if he remembered Orson or Dora. He might (aged 12) have received candy from me at the panegyri. Had he? He looked doubtful. I wasn't communicating. Kosta & Maritsa, oh yes, them he had known; they were now in Athens. As for O.—

"The brother you," said George, "no good man."

"Oh? *Why?*" (A word I now use all the time, mimicking G. It is our little joke.)

"Kyrios Yannis (the E. C.) speak no good."

"Kyrios Yannis is wrong." I showed him *wrong* in my dictionary.

George snickered. "Kyrios Yannis is——." (A word I forget & would not have understood out of context.)

He is a bundle of prejudice. I gathered yesterday that he has no use for Chryssoula. Why? Because she is not a Dibliotissa, but from depraved Rhodes. (C. calls *him* uno teddy-boy, he might care to know.)

We talked a lot about girls. Unmarried Greek girls do not go All The Way. George confessed that Inge was his 2nd *real* experience.

"Only the second?" I looked surprised. "*Why?*"

"Never mind," he grinned. "I am Greek." (!!)

Another hot day. The hollows of the miniature waves were black. They slid onto the beach with the sound of water-drops striking a red-hot skillet.

I didn't go to Byron's yesterday. We would have talked about O., I could feel it in my bones—or in my blood which by now is only a bare degree thicker than water. It is not thicker than ouzo; my tongue would have wagged disloyally. Disloyalty partly to Orson (where can he be?); mainly to Orestes, who gasps in these pages.

The modern Greek language can be said to have suffered a stroke. Vowels, the full *oi*'s & *ei*'s of classical days, have been eclipsed to a waning, whin-
Dora's      ing *ee*. Obsessive jumbling of consonants in
amnesia    the dark. Speech of a brilliant, impaired mind. A crime committed in the name of Grimm's Law.

15.vii.61
The boat, white, graceful, is floated not in water but some insubstantial
      rather in an ultra-violet light against a background of heavy black & gold-green cliffs, ferned ledges for birds to nest on. A real place?
      There shall be no more travel, only the Voyage. Is that the message? Voyage (as if derived from *voir*): a Seeing.

The boat at least *is* real. It is the N.'s caïque, a watercolor of it by Lucine which I claimed today at the postoffice. Postmarked illegibly. Am I to guess that she can be found aboard, that stroke of orange against the railing?

It is the voyage not made. The boat missed.

I could *be* a castaway, with my 9-day beard & faded shirt. Shall I be discovered at the water's edge, shirt tied to the oar I brandish, croaking in a half forgotten tongue: I'm here! Rescue me!

Or later, telling the tale: I was seven lean years on that island. With only a ~~notebook~~ parrot for company.

By the time they reach Paris, Sandy is sick again. They take ~~me~~ him to the American Hospital. The doctor assures them that diet & rest will do the trick. No need for alarm, or for O. & D. to stay. They can't afford to, at any rate. O. must resume teaching in September. Sandy promises to follow. If they had waited for him— But life became easy, opened out in strange directions he was too young, too curious not to investigate. He meets (Marianne). The letters from Houston ignored. Now he is through college, if he goes home he will only be taken into the Army. All this 7 years ago next month. It is 1 1/2 years before he returns to America & then not for long. Marianne has found him a job as tutor to her little nephews.

As this isn't Sandy's story, I could take out his jaundice altogether when I start to write. Let him

vanish into the Orient as planned, while Orestes &
Dora proceed from Italy to Paris—making in reverse
my final trip with M. (all in that winter's notebooks).
The 2 situations much alike—younger man, older
woman; monuments, arguments, a love outlived.

Or did the jaundice mix its yellow with the blue of
those far-off slopes        rustling of new green
Unless that youthful jaundice
indispensable ~~yellow~~ primary color added to the
blues of those lost days, turning them
The savage beak & idiot green wings
Full of my words, the notebook flapped its pages—

24.vii.61
I woke in the small hours, a sharp weight on my
chest. It was Chryssoula's cat, motors purring, claws
kneading me through the sheet. I guessed rather than
saw the dilated shining eyes fixed upon me. Instead of
chasing it away, though, I began mumbling gently in
response—"Good kitty, proud, loyal, generous Cat"—
generous!—& other nonsense words until my eyes filled
with tears to think that only then, in the middle of the
night, rinsed by sleep and with only an animal for company, could I discover words of love. I stroked the
strange, cool fur. Good, proud, loyal, who was I addressing if not this loving self of mine that had woken,
that was digging its claws lightly, voluptuously into my
flesh? It wasn't comfortable, frankly. I had to shift in
bed. The cat jumped to the floor, then to the window-
sill, then out. A few feet to the left is a balcony that gives

onto the corridor. I lay back dreaming of day, of Orson, Lucine, R. in Venice, M. in Tangier, of my mother & father, of those New York scenes I am trying to compose without opening this notebook; of the love & sweetness I had woken brimming with, and how I might nurse it, keep it from draining out of my cupped hands into dust before it reached its proper objects—O. & L. & the rest, or even (lacking them) the pages of my novel. But of course I had only to think these thoughts in order to feel the threat, then the reality, of their withdrawal. It would seem that love, ἀγάπη, lives by its own laws, like a cat, & will not be commanded.

## PART ~~II~~ III ~~?~~
*(A Fair Copy)*

They reached New York on an August morning.
Arthur Orson had written to Paris, after no little de-
liberation, offering his guest room for a week or so until
they found a flat of their own. Nearly seventy now, a
bachelor to boot, his hesitation was natural. Orestes'
letter told him worse than nothing regarding This
Woman, as Arthur called Dora in a number of dialogues with his better nature. Who was she, and how
*much* older than Orestes? Of just what society, please,
was she the "cream"? He could hardly trust his godson's judgment in these matters. Arthur was no prude;
if they weren't married, it didn't concern him. But, set
in his ways, fussy and autocratic from the years spent
with nobody to please but himself, he did not exactly
look forward to roughing it, high up there in the grand
scenery of other people's lives.

The past took over, though. For minutes at a time
he was young again, it was thirty-five years earlier, and
the letter tucked in his engagement book was not from
Orestes but Orestes' father, announcing *his* arrival, with
Eleni and the baby, in New York. The annoyance and
curiosity felt then as now (who was This Woman? what
business had his friend, or godson, involving himself
with her, with any woman? She came from a higher
class, did she? Hmf! How would *he* know?) gave Arthur

the sense that his total personality was smoothly, intelligently functioning. "If I know anything," he told his better nature, "I know the world, its pitfalls and deceptions. They never ask *me* when they make their rash decisions, but you'll see. After one year with this woman, he'll come whining to me, his only friend, just mark my words." Thirty-five years ago, of course, Arthur had done everything in his power to help Orestes' father, found him work, found them lodgings, sent them food, paid for the doctors, the hospital, the funeral of that wonderful, strong, good man. In Arthur's bedroom stood a framed photograph of himself posing with his friend before a whitewashed house. It had been taken on a Sunday in 1915. Both were wearing dark suits and tieless white shirts buttoned at the collar. Orestes' father would have been in his early twenties; he was looking superbly at the camera from behind a thick, curling moustache. Arthur Orson had been, of all things, a spy in the First War. During the Gallipoli Campaign he had met Orestes' father, had in fact been hidden for a month in his house, in his room. "He saved my life," he would say aloud, letting the magic work. "I was ill, he cared for me like a brother. His memory is sacred to me to this day."

"And Eleni?" asked Arthur's better nature, one of whose favorite stories it was.

"Agh. She remarried, miraculously."

"Why so? Wasn't she still very lovely?"

"Yes, perhaps. But a shrew. She drove him to his death."

"Oh? It wasn't cancer, then?"

"Am I expected to remember everything? Whatever it was, he died, Eleni remarried, and my little namesake—he was given Orson as a second name, you recall—went off with her to far-away Texas."

They had kept in touch, but Arthur did not see his godson again until he was thirty and a Professor, with degrees.

To the surprise of both, they became friends. Each probably amused the other by his inexperience. Arthur went so far as to enroll in one of Orestes' night classes for adults. Words like 'antithesis' or 'metaphysical', or sentences beginning 'The poet in his lonely search for belief . . .' made his eyes shift nervously, but he enjoyed the relish with which Orestes could utter them. Afterwards would come a removal to somebody's apartment, wine and cookies, more talk. One night Tennyson was mentioned. "Oh," said Orestes at once, "an extraordinary technician but a minor poet. It is hard for me to feel his greatness." Wasn't 'In Memoriam' a great poem? "The poem he wrote for Arthur Hallam," Orestes began, pausing because of the other Arthur in his audience, whom he wanted to savor the pleasant coincidence of names; "Tennyson's friend who died young," he went on, and now met Arthur's eyes, reminded of his similar loss (which was, to be sure, Orestes' own as well)—"Yes, perhaps 'In Memoriam' is a great poem. A sensibility as delicate as Tennyson's could draw from a friend's death insights analogous to those of the saint in contemplation of Christ's passion.

These insights are all the more poignant for contemporary readers like ourselves, for whom the Christian myth has fallen to pieces. Only a supreme artist in our day can solder them together. You will understand how I feel about 'In Memoriam' if you compare it with Eliot's magnificent *collage* of faith and faiths—Tennyson on the one hand, content to echo the cadences of Anglican hymns; Eliot on the other, aware in his sophistication that the fragments he has 'shored up' are valid *because* of their flaws, their inefficacy as living doctrine—" Enough. Orestes' talk popped with allusion and paradox. It was like sitting by a fire. At the evening's end Arthur breathed the cool of his own life gratefully.

From him Orestes learned—no, Orestes never learned. He lacked skill and patience to help work the crazy-quilt of amenity and obligation that was the older man's daily life. Everything Arthur did related to others. Even in museums he stood longest in front of paintings whose previous owners he had known—Miss A.'s Manet, Lord B.'s Crivelli. On the way out he would stop to say hello to one of the curators. Months later he took Orestes to dinner in this man's apartment. Orestes was the only guest not in evening clothes. He soon found, furthermore, that his discourse curdled the bland flow of talk and gossip. Before long he was listening in appalled fascination, beyond speech as the others were beyond thought—for so he unjustly dismissed them, blind to the intense thought behind the flowers, the china, the menu, and deaf to the truth of any remark clever enough to make him smile. Here Orestes was close, as Arthur pointed out, to contradicting himself. What was this cleverness if not a kind of poetry? Didn't his own lectures sparkle with it? Ah, but no—Orestes' lectures were about serious things. Poetry, for Arthur, might be cleverness, mere icing on the cake; for Orestes it was a way of life. "Believe me," said his friend, "so is cleverness. By the way your manners are improving. You didn't fold your napkin when you got up from table."

It was Aesop's fox and stork all over again. Arthur lapped a bit from the top of the jar; Orestes stabbed guardedly at the shallow dish. Their partings were warm with relief. And when Orestes finally sailed for Greece, Arthur gave him a larger check than he had intended.

At last the doorbell rang. Here they were. As he hastened to admit them, Arthur's numerous misgivings about Dora shrank to one childish prayer: "Let her be able to appreciate me, let her see that I have taste!"

His living room was painted dark red and ivory. It had one antiqued-mirror wall, a piano (Arthur had resumed his lessons, after fifty-five years), velvet chairs, gladiolas in silver vases. There were many Greek objects: amber rosaries, a good ikon, and some large, prominently hung sepia photographs of sculpture—the Charioteer, the Hermes at Olympia, the Ephebe at Constantinople. Indeed, Dora exclaimed with pleasure. She did feel at home, she had had no idea from Orestes that one could be so comfortable in New York; so that, with no further thought given to the qualms each had felt with respect to the other (for Dora, too, had begun to sprinkle large grains of salt on Orestes' judgments of people), she and Arthur sat down, vastly pleased with their mutual surfaces, to Turkish coffee and a sweet on a spoon. Orestes, overexcited, paced the room. They watched him indulgently, like parents whose child has come home.

Arthur, a little man, sallow and vain, with a mole on his forehead and eyebrows long as antennae, was presently dreaming of taking her over, introducing her as *his* friend and sharing in the invitations she would receive. Orestes wanted her to see *things*; he had been picturing her excitement in zoos, on the top of skyscrapers, in the subway. Dora obliged them both.

Within a few days she had been to Chinatown, Bloomingdales, the Frick, Staten Island, had watched TV and been given an evening party. Arthur spent most of that day polishing silver candlesticks, washing long-stemmed glasses he hadn't used for months, and arranging flowers. "You've gone to too much trouble," said Orestes, inwardly delighted, on his return with Dora from their apartment-hunt. Arthur merely shrugged. He knew no other way to give a party. Certainly the surer thing was to prepare one's background, order things to eat, serve champagne—domestic, if need be—in thin crystal, than to rely on kind words and gestures. What if the heart were not inspired to warmth, the tongue to liveliness? One must provide against that kind of failure. And the party, considering that most of the people Arthur knew were dead or out of town for the summer, went off quite passably. Nothing was broken. The handful of Bohemians invited by Orestes stayed too late but otherwise behaved. Cold cuts and petits fours remained which would do for Arthur's lunch the next day. And he felt that *his* guests (the museum director, the piano teacher, ten all told) had got the point of Dora. Despite her costume.

Orestes had had her wear an ankle-length black lace dress, old yet in itself becoming. Then, horrors! minutes before the first arrivals, he opened a paper bag and took out a yard of broad crimson moiré ribbon. This he draped Dora with, diagonally, like some ambassadorial decoration fastened by pins at shoulder and hip, and at the breast by a brooch of her own. It cost Arthur an effort to smile and say nothing, as Dora herself did, and wait for the first person to whom Orestes introduced her as the "Greek Ambassadress" to see the joke before he, Arthur, allowed himself to remark that fun was fun but decorations were decorations.

Dora would have agreed with him on a different occasion, but she felt more warmly toward Orestes now than she had in the weeks before they reached New York, and she had resolved to take pleasure in whatever made him happy. Watching him in relation to Arthur, it gratified her to see, as with Orestes and his brother, that two highly dissimilar individuals were drawing closer through her, and was European enough to wonder, where Arthur was concerned—an elderly man, without heirs—if this increased closeness mightn't lead to something rather agreeable for Orestes. For herself, she objected not one bit to dressing up as grander than she was. We all dream of coming back from the Flea Market with a Fragonard. If Orestes wanted to have brought from Europe something more than an old island woman, she would lend herself to his plot, she would impersonate the fabulous souvenir. Meanwhile, her eyes had been open. Beginning with that green, torch-bearing giantess in the harbor, all militant wakefulness compared to her sleeping, natural sister viewed from Diblos, Dora had taken in a type of New York woman—in the street, in the pages of *Vogue*—angular, high-heeled, hatless, being dragged hilarious down the pavement by a huge shaven dog, or squinting heavenwards with a look of utter, harrowed anxiety which must be, in this city at least, as much beauty's indispensable earmark as an enigmatic smile had been in Leonardo's Italy. It was not a type Dora cared to resemble. Yet she already knew, from being dragged down pavements by Orestes, something of what lay in the heart of the woman with the poodle, and beneath Dora's tanned, lined face and fingers placidly, clumsily mending a tear in the black lace dress, had already appeared the psychic counterparts of furrowed brow, strained, painted mouth, knuckles clenched white—all ignored, all nonetheless ready for use at the first proof of her own total folly to have considered (at her age!) making a life among the barbarians.

There, then, she stood among them, the Ambassadress, sipping the Great Western champagne. Compared to her, the others were friendlier, better informed, more intense, or more talkative; her failure in these respects seemed rather to strengthen her position. To have been European *and* immensely charming might have been more than the company could bear. She raised her glass to Orestes across the room.

His eyes had been on her. It had just entered his head to have her talk to his mother on the telephone. In Greek, naturally! "What a good idea," said Dora. Soon she was called into Arthur's bedroom. Eleni, in Texas, was already on the line and Orestes—talking English— had finished what he had to say. Dora found herself uttering a tentative "Hello" into the receiver. "Talk Greek! Talk Greek!" cried Orestes. She did so, found easily a number of cordial phrases, mentioned her fondness for both Eleni's sons, hoped before long to know *her* as well—but then, as Eleni replied, it became plain, with every allowance for fluster, that Greek was no longer a tongue she could speak to any useful degree. It made no difference; Dora slipped back into English, remarked the extent of Eleni's, modified her own to suit it, and so ended the conversation.

"She sounds *very* nice," she told Orestes. "I should love to know her. What an absorbing life that must be!" He, however, dragged her back to the party. "I couldn't believe it!" he told group after group. "My mother can't speak Greek any more! I was amazed! She and I speak English together—*my* Greek was lousy before I went to Greece. But imagine! She's forgotten it! And her English isn't fluent, is it, Dora? Do you see what that means? My mother has no language!"

"There must be more important things in life," said Dora, embarrassed. He had made it sound very dire.

"Than language?"

"Than languages, surely."

"That coming from you who speak four perfectly! Ha ha!" cried Orestes throwing his arms around her and her enhanced value. People did that in America, she had noticed, though he had now gone on to tell some others how physical the Greeks were, how they couldn't talk without touching or hugging each other. "Yes," said Dora, "but you're talking of a certain class. Tasso could never bear to be touched, neither could Byron, even as a child." But anything she said made him like her more. "You see," his smile told the room, "she knows, she's the genuine article."

That evening, for the first time in their friendship, Orestes became "an American" in Dora's eyes. She glimpsed the larger, national mystery behind his manners, that pendulum swinging from childish artlessness to artless maturity and back again. She welcomed the insight gaily, secure in her resiliency. When the museum director, saying goodnight, promised to telephone in the morning to give her the name of "a really dependable rug man" through whom to sell her Bokhara, she begged him not to go out of his way. "Oh well, yes, the rug must be sold eventually, but I won't have my friends feeling responsible for me. I'd be happy on the corner with a cart full of apples!"

Dora and Orestes found an apartment, no floor of a brownstone house, as recommended by Arthur and which was available at great cost (unless in such poor condition as to remind Orestes of the primal tenement he was still running away from); instead, three rooms in a new, mountainous "development" overlooking the East River. It had a uniformed doorman—whom Orestes trained, without letting him in on the joke, to call Dora 'Baroness'—and a lobby decorated by Dorothy Draper. There was Musak in the self-operated elevators. The river-front apartments, it turned out, cost ten dollars per room more each month than those facing other tall buildings. "We'll know the river's there," Dora said.

On the eighteenth floor they had plenty of light. Their living room was too large, the bedroom and kitchen too small. When it came to furniture, Orestes developed a violent phobia of anything second-hand, so that for their first dinner at home they drew two shiny metal and leatherette chairs up to a vinyl-topped cardtable. Dora switched off a three-headed lamp. Candlelight richened the Bokhara and blurred a pattern of orange and green boomerangs on the sofa-bed and the wall to wall, ceiling to floor draperies installed that day against the cruel afternoon glare. The friends drank to their new home. It was costing a lot but they had done it, it was theirs, and Orestes, for one, felt that these new, durable, practical possessions would save expense in the long run. Three months passed. The chair seats were cracking to reveal gray cotton wadding, somebody's cigarette had blistered the table. The Bokhara was still on the floor but the curtains did not close, or the bed open, properly, and Dora was working as a governess in New Jersey.

It was better than it sounded. The family was Dutch, the daughters twelve and fourteen. Dora walked them to school, returned to the house, made a bed or two, ate on a tray with the grandfather in his room, read, fetched the girls, took one to her music lesson and did Greek or Italian conversation with the other. The family dined together, Dora with them. Both parents were translators at the United Nations. On weekends Dora was free to join Orestes.

She tried not to feel it as an obligation, those Friday evenings, reentering the apartment. She was paying her share, true; but more and more it seemed, as she gave him the money each month, that she was buying her own privacy from Orestes. For two nights he would move onto the sofa-bed, giving up the bedroom to her. On one night they would go to the theatre; on the other, receive friends. It soon appeared that these sleeping arrangements were unsatisfactory. The weekend found Dora refreshed, ready for the diversions it was thought better to have earned, in America, than mere money; while Orestes, exhausted by work, face green and long as the face in an ikon, might have been happy to slip into his relinquished bedroom somewhat before the last guests had left.

To his regular lectures had been added a weekly TV program, "The World of Poetry." Produced with a

minimum of fuss over an educational channel, at the
wrong hour of the wrong evening, it nevertheless by
spring had gathered a faithful public who wrote letters,
telephoned the station, sent Orestes their photographs
and sonnets. He took it all very seriously. Wearing a
new pale blue shirt, he had arrived for his debut an hour
early, ready to put himself in the hands of the cosmeti-
cians. There were none. His disappointment, though
concealed, was justified; on the screen he looked unwell
and weird. His programs tended to fall into two halves:
the classic, the contemporary. After an initial talk on,
say, Shelley, with resonant quotation prefaced by sips
of water, he would try to wind up with "a Shelley of
today"—some odd young man he would have met, who
was meant to give the viewers an absolutely authentic
image of genius struggling from the chrysalis of society.
Orestes relied perhaps too heavily upon his friends to
perform, rather than poets whose names were better
known. But the public seemed ill-equipped to tell the
difference. So much so that, today in New York, these
discoveries of Orestes, published by now and with their
own disciples, make up a clearly defined battalion in
the endless literary wars of our time.

There was the film, too. In these months Orestes
was writing the first of six complete scripts. A week in
Hollywood, the frequent telephone conferences there-
after, had not helped him form a notion of how to proceed. Each month, when the producer came to town, a
big black car would call for Orestes and sweep him, in
evening clothes at first rented, eventually his very own,

into the countryside for a party with starlets and big-
wigs. From one such dinner, near Christmas, he returned with a pair of gold and sapphire cufflinks. It was
hard to resist, for Orestes, a little gentle namedropping;
and, for others, a little gentle irony at his expense. Certain young poets—infants in Dora's eyes—so devoted to
their calling as never to have heard of selling one's
talents, dipped into the punchbowl and came up with
a hesitant question. Wasn't that what Orestes was doing? Wasn't his time too precious for this kind of
drudgery?

He would admit it himself some days. He rose at
seven, never retired before midnight.

Only once, one miserable midweek night before
Dora had found work, did she and Orestes try a Greek
restaurant. A new one had opened near Times Square,
and the idea had been to go forth, a company of poets,
to taste the richly restorative food and society of Greeks.

The place seemed large and crowded. They were
put at a recently vacated table.

"This is strange," said Orestes, moving his face
about. "Can you *see*, Dora?"

The lighting was dim but might not have existed,
to hear him talk. "I've never seen a Greek restaurant,"
he went on, "that wasn't a blaze of electric light. The
Greeks love light. In Athens, in broad daylight, the
the butcher stalls are outlined and festooned with
lighted bulbs. They are theatres in which brains and
hearts have literally been laid bare, all buzzing with

flies. And the crowds!" He asked their waiter in Greek, good-naturedly, why it was so dark in the restaurant.

"How's everybody tonight?" said the waiter, re-moving soiled napkins and glasses. "A cocktail before your meal, folks?"

Dora wanted a Manhattan. Orestes told the young poets to try ouzo, then repeated his question in English.

"You got me," came the answer. "Unless it's the ladies. They often like not too bright a room." He handed round red and gold menus.

"It's true," said Dora, "you see very few women eating out in Athens, except in summer. Here, every-one's brought his wife along."

"Wait," said Orestes to the waiter. "What part of Greece are you from?"

Eager to leave, the waiter admitted Sparta.

"But you don't speak Greek? I'm amazed!"

"Oh, I'm Greek, I speak Greek!" and with a smile of reassurance he escaped.

"That was childish of me," Orestes laughed. "But he should be prouder of his heritage."

As he peered into the dim hubbub, Orestes said goodbye to any hopes of reliving those brilliant evenings in taverns across the water. The crossing itself had wrought a sea-change upon the other Greek customers. Young men who, on native ground a few years earlier, would have listened to Orestes with dreaming eyes had already watched dream after dream sinking into a parody of its fulfillment: fortune, family, the wife to dress (or overdress), the child to educate (or worse, since

this was America, to be educated *by*)—and all these lives
at once insured, reflected, and corroded by conven-
iences bought on time, in time, *with* time, payments the
receipts for which could be examined even here,
through smoke, in the form of sallow, untended flesh
and the delusive mannerisms of the insider. Dante
might have spoken to these diners, gone over the receipts, shown them where they had paid too much; not
Orestes. With a shudder of horror and identification he
turned back to his party.

"No, but really," Dora remarked when he had said
his piece, "you'll see the same class of people in Athens,
if you know where to look."

"I give you the light of Greece, then," smiled Orestes, lifting his glass. "Once you have had your vision, no
lesser world is altogether tolerable. I used to enjoy
places like this. But I've been *there*, I've felt the sun
licking at my wings. If I were Icarus, I would set out
tomorrow—to melt in that sun, to drown in that sea!"

At least they would have a good meal. Turning to
the menu, Orestes ordered portions of souvlakia,
moussaka, stuffed vine-leaves—ah, and there were
calamarákia! Nothing was more delicious (he told the
poets) than these little squid, crisp with golden batter.
Did they come from Florida? The waiter couldn't say.
"Well, two portions of those," said Orestes. "And of
course, wine."

"I'll bring the wine list," said the waiter, by now
speaking Greek to oblige him.

"Don't bother. Just two large cans of retsina."

"We have only bottled wine."

"Bottles then," said Orestes with an indifferent wave of his hand.

The bouzoukia orchestra, which had been resting when their party arrived, began to play. Eight men sat in a row, gazing nowhere and deftly worrying their instruments. A soloist advanced to the edge of the platform. Her body, barely contained by a white and silver dress, might have been artificially matured so as to be recognizable as female at immense distances. Black, platinum-streaked curls spilled onto fat shoulders and quivering arms. She held a cloth orchid concealing a microphone. By turns sweet, hoarse, piercing, dripping with ornaments and imperfections, her voice reached them as an aural equivalent of the many-layered, honey-soaked baclava Orestes intended ordering for dessert. This much, surely, was authentic—or was it? One poet thought he recognized an Italian hit of the year before.

Nobody got up to dance. "But nobody's dancing— why?" asked Orestes when the waiter brought their orders.

"It is not permitted."

A plate set before Orestes seemed to contain five or six fingers, swollen purplish-pink and trailing oil-black roots. What was this? His calamarákia.

"Ah no. I wanted them fried. I've never seen squid served this way. They're not even hot. Take them away, ask the cook to fry them properly."

The waiter removed the two portions.

A second song ended to loud applause. The singer blew one kiss and ambled pouting from the stage. "One likes her," Orestes explained, "because she is the essence of voluptuous femininity." Then he noticed that the vine-leaves had come out of a can. He could tell by a certain green dye mixed with the oil. "As a rule I don't let trivial details upset me," he said. "It's not like me to lodge complaints—is it, Dora?"

It was not, and she said so.

"Forgive me, then, if I do this once. It will be for the glory that was Greece."

So the drama moved inexorably to its close. The wine was wrong. The same calamarákia returned, perhaps hotter. Meanwhile, a child-faced poet had been made unwell by a single glass of ouzo. The waiter offered to show Orestes the brine-vat in the kitchen, out of which the wine-leaves had been taken. Orestes waved him away, calling for the manager.

"Oríste!" cried this person when he appeared.

"He knows you . . . ?" the sick poet moaned, mistaking for Orestes' name the conventional Greek reply to a summons.

"I ordered fresh calamarákia, fried," began Orestes. The manager regretted; there was no fresh squid at this time of year. Then why had it been on the menu? Ah, the menu did not say *fresh* squid. Here as in any Greek restaurant, one basic menu did for all seasons. And some people preferred their squid canned, yes indeed! The two portions in question, however, would not appear on their check.

This concession failed to satisfy Orestes.

"Another thing," he said, shifting to English. "This wine tastes funny, and the ouzo can't have been good. It has made my friend ill."

The manager took a sip of wine, then looked closely at the poet. "He's under age, isn't he? Did he show any identification?"

"I'm surprised you can see him at all in this light!"

"Look, Sir, don't blame me for the New York State Law. I'm just the guy who gets his permit taken away."

"This is ridiculous," said Orestes. "No Greek has ever

Dream—Venice, a Hospital. O. is to undergo surgery. Reception desk very crowded. Old woman edges in front of him. I make her yield her place & try to tell the nurse O.'s name. We are separated at the elevators. Mine: a moving wooden room like a rustic privy. Hot sun through a knothole burns my wrist (redder & hairier than mine) & I think, Summer at last! Now we move sideways like a train. At the end of a vast streaked palazzo (the Hosp.) I get off. I wear black trousers, black turtleneck, am barefoot. While I wait for O., an attendant—older, heavy accent—talks to me. He cannot believe I'm born in Texas, says there's something 'Italian' about the back of my head. I say, conscious of speaking a highly artificial language, "Perhaps I have foreign blood." He: Beg pardon—what? I: Foreign blood. He: Foreign *what?* "BLOOD!" I shout. And O. comes limping into view.

come within five years of guessing an American's age."

"I am nineteen," declared the poet haughtily.

"I'm not asking for the gentleman's word," said the manager. "I'm asking to see his driver's license."

"I don't drive."

"It's a matter of principle," said a second poet, beginning to laugh.

Orestes struck the table lightly with his palm. Until now, only his Greek pride had been offended. But the appeal to local ordinances aroused an American dander he hadn't known he had. "Ask the waiter to bring our check."

The manager hesitated. Suppose these were well-connected people? In that brief interval Dora spoke up.

She *didn't* feel like leaving, did they mind? She put her hand on Orestes' and smiled up at the manager. If they could just have some bicarbonate of soda? she said in her plainest, most motherly Greek. It was wet out, the rest of the dinner was so good! "Orestes, you must try my moussaka, they've given me far too much."

It worked. The manager melted away. Orestes let himself be calmed.

The worst, from her point of view, was simply to have lost control in front of the young. Luckily they were poets. Abstracter topics presented themselves, the music continued to please, the baclava was a success. So, perhaps, was the evening as a whole, in every mind but Orestes'. Into him the half averted scene kept biting deeply. What had he expected? Greece in America? He was not used to this grinding confusion of loyalties.

Either, it seemed, one was Greek and unfortified against the virus endemic here, or American and a carrier. The two natures absolutely did not mix. To emerge at last, twenty dollars poorer, onto the neon-streaked, puddle-paved streets came as no relief. People of every description jostled them. It was the melting-pot with a vengeance. Dora took his arm and led him, the poets following, calmly through the flashing, shrieking labyrinth. She seemed actually to know where they were.

More and more she was coming to baffle a possessiveness he felt for her. From the start it had been of absurd yet paramount importance that she *see* and *feel* New York. After her maiden trip on the subway, he had turned to her, ready for superlatives. But what was Dora to say who had ridden the Métro a month before, who had gone by train under the Alps, for that matter? This was no typically 'New York' experience. Orestes looked away in frustration. The contest recurred daily. She had *been* in department stores, she had already tasted doughnuts. She had seen crowds almost as huge crawling at the bottom of chasms less deep, perhaps, than these—but she was no judge of depth. The Louvre allowed her to be critical of the Metropolitan, the Comédie of Broadway. Orestes could teach her nothing. It was as if his very virility were being challenged. Wasn't there something, he asked one day with desperate lightness, something singular about his home-town that had struck her, that she hadn't foreseen? "Ah yes!" she exclaimed, then had to think. "Well, there are many more Negroes than I'd imagined. And many more antique shops."

Reluctantly he evolved the theory that it was too much for her. No woman her age could cope with a world so drastically at odds with all she had known. Her serenity was a defense, a symptom of shock. Neither then nor later when events bore it out did this view of Dora comfort him.

The matter of her finding work arose, horrifying Orestes. He had no claims, could not forbid her (his former hostess, now less than a guest) to look for a job. So he retreated into a childish coldness—let her just try independence, she would see her folly—broken by spells of frenzied rationality, budgets littering the vinyl table, aimed at keeping her by his side.

Dora had taken to going to Arthur Orson's for tea every few days. Here her instinct was applauded. New York without a job could be a living hell—ask him, the idle old man chuckled, he ought to know. They put their heads together over the difficulties. She had come to America on a visitor's, not a worker's, visa—which by the way was due to expire in three months. She could renew it for another six, and would no doubt be quite ready for repatriation at the end of them. "But suppose I'm not," she asked Arthur, "suppose I want never to leave?"

"Then you will simply have to stay."

"It's not that simple. I should have to marry an American." She was joking. "Can you picture it? At my age?"

Arthur looked at his chrysanthemums.

"Why not marry me?" he finally said.

When she told Orestes, he went all to pieces. "You aren't serious," he kept saying.

Dora asked if he could think of a more suitable arrangement.

"I wasn't aware that your fondness for my country had reached such a pitch," he said with the elegance of hurt feelings. "Or should I take it as a personal compliment?"

"If you like, my dear," she replied gently. "Or think of it as self-indulgence." She let her hand rest upon one of that year's anxiety-packed headlines. "I might not care to live through another war in Greece."

"But with Arthur!"

"Really, Orestes. It would be a marriage of convenience. We'd live apart. Nothing's settled in any case. All Arthur did was to bring up the possibility."

"You'd go on living here with me? Would that look proper?"

"Does it look proper now?"

"This once, Dora, don't be witty, I beg you. Marriage is a human sacrament," said he who knew nothing about it. "I'm profoundly shocked to know that you would consider Arthur as a husband."

She saw then and there that it would have to be Orestes whom she married.

Arguments came to support this daring notion. Under scrutiny the margin of years between them changed into an advantage. Arthur, despite his talk of living apart, was old and fragile; age could turn overnight into helplessness. As his wife—for Dora also took marriage seriously, having had thirty-eight years of it with Tasso—she would run the risk of becoming his companion, his nurse. No thank you! Then, Arthur's world. It was too close to Athens society—small, elderly, proper; a little went a long way. She had developed a taste for long bare avenues, glass buildings the light bounced off. With Orestes, now that the dawning on the terrace at Diblos lay behind her and, believe it or not as he pleased, no shred of longing remained, it seemed to Dora that this love overcome—if it had been love, there was no saying now—had earned her certain rights, that he owed her compensation, as if she had hurt herself in his service. And she, why, she owed it to him to marry him! Who had wanted her here? Who had escorted her to this huge, glittering American function? It went against her upbringing to desert him now. No, while the chandeliers blazed, she was under Orestes' protection; while the music played, she would face it at his side.

They exchanged vows and rings in a civil service in January. This time, at the party Arthur gave, the champagne was imported.

That night, a Saturday, Orestes, dressed in red silk pyjamas, knocked on the bedroom door. He was now The Bridegroom; he would have knocked at a cotton-gin's door if he had just been married to one. As it was, his feelings for Dora had deepened and widened under

~~A miserable moment. Returning unexpectedly af-~~
~~ter starting for the beach, I found Chryssoula in my~~
~~room. Cleaning? Something crackled guiltily, she was~~
~~thrusting her hand into her blouse. I thought of the 500~~
~~drachma note hidden in this book. I questioned her.~~
~~She showed her empty hands. I asked what was hidden~~
~~in her blouse. Nothing! I knew she was lying. Suddenly~~
~~she was in a fury. You think I'm a thief, search me!~~
~~Eyes blazing. She seized my hand & thrust it into her~~
~~bosom where, along with everything else, was indeed a~~
~~square of paper. It was my passport photo; there had~~
~~been several in an envelope in my drawer. C. was in~~
~~tears. I wanted to comfort her. Her lips compressed,~~
~~she turned proudly aside. Now she has left. My image~~
~~lies curled & damp on the table. "Sei bello," she said,~~
~~"ma non hai cuore." The lagoon shimmers. The torso~~
~~lies outstretched at its far end. The money was of course~~
~~safe between these two blank pages. Her scent is on the~~
~~palm I raise to hide my face. "The only solution is to~~
~~be very, very intelligent."~~

the spell of having a sacramental role to perform. He
had also drunk wine. Their relationship seemed to him
one of infinite possibility.

    She was still up and about, in her hairnet and old
blue wrapper. "How smart you look," she said, missing
the import of his appearance.

    "I wanted you to see that I was proud to be your
husband," said Orestes, smiling.

    "Thank you, my dear. I'm very happy too."

"Let me kiss you good night, Dora."

"Good night, Orestes." She gave him her roughened cheek. He held her a moment, weighing her unreadiness.

"Dora . . . ?"

She drew back. When she raised her eyes it was in a slow look brimming with comfort. She pressed his hand, then let go gently. Speechless, he took his leave.

Man and wife at last, their relationship was virtually at an end. No scenes, no recriminations, only this gradual firm gentleness on Dora's part, and the difficulty of meeting her eyes for long. Who did meet those eyes, or what? The Dutch family's cat. A stand of yellow, shuddering bamboo in a southerly angle of their house. Gray skies. Windows reflected in water.

One morning in March she discovered herself walking along a canal, an embankment anyhow, shining with frost and strewn with rusted fragments of machinery. It would have been quite early. The sun, low and mild, startled her, now in the sky, now glancing off the windows of a warehouse opposite. "But what am I doing here?" she said to herself in Italian. "Tasso will be furious."

She tried to concentrate upon the cryptic litter of metal. A filthy yellow dog squatted in its midst, trembling violently; risen, it sniffed the steaming earth. When it turned to her, she saw a fresh wound on its head. "Cosa vuoi?" she asked it in a sweet, croaking voice, her hand held out appealingly. The air had grown warmer. Smells reached her; it was spring. The dog, grinning like a shark, had not moved. She walked deeper into the scene.

Later she was extremely tired. The police had odd uniforms and spoke English. She answered what she could of their questions. Her name? She gave it calmly. Yes, married; there was the ring on her finger. She told them Tasso's name and where they lived. Was that in New Jersey? Doubt must have crossed her face. Next, they wanted to know what year it was. Really, how stupid! But she couldn't tell from their faces whether her answer was right or wrong. She begged their pardon, adding that she had had little or no sleep. The coffee they gave her was weak but delicious.

In the next room an officer was saying, ". . . Yes, come on down. . . . Legally, you understand, we ought to. . . . Yes . . . all right . . . O. K."

Soon a fair woman who spoke French arrived at the police station, and kissed her. When Dora had not returned last night (the woman said) they had telephoned Orestes to find out if she had missed her train. Whom had they telephoned? Never mind. Hush. The panic was over, they had found her. A doctor was waiting to see her. Hush. Come.

Dora's amnesia disappeared by evening and never recurred. The doctor saw her several times. He asked, had there been any recent shock or upheaval in her life? She told him no.

Orestes said, "Ah, Dora, I understand these things. It's me you're trying to forget. You want to blot out everything that has to do with me."

Arthur said, "If *my* memory went, where would I be? Who would look after me? The very thought sends chills."

On her next weekend in New York, Dora went to a hotel.

Shame was what *she* felt. To be found wandering, a derelict; anything might have happened. To be faced with the frailty of one's reason, there among the rusted parts, the filth, in a glare that assailed one like the dog's gaze, wherever one turned. As she stripped these painful details of a certain prismatic beauty that had overlaid them at the time, she recognized in their poverty, their menace, more and more of her situation with Orestes. Her shame widened to include this, too.

She felt she had had the narrowest of escapes.

"I shall go back to Greece," she said aloud to the hotel wallpaper. But her mistake, if it was one, seemed at once too grave and too recent to acknowledge by such a step.

"If it were not for Byron," she told a tired, sympathetic face in the mirror.

On Sunday she forced herself to visit the apartment.

"Good evening, Baroness," said the doorman.

"Dora!" exclaimed Orestes dramatically. "Are you all right? I've been terribly anxious. We all have. Arthur just phoned. I've had no sleep—"

She pressed his hand, nodding. It was the morning on the terrace, only he had slipped into her role. Well, he was welcome to it.

"We thought it must be another attack of amnesia."

"No."

"Where have you been, then? Arthur was calling the hospitals."

She explained and begged his pardon.

"Give me your coat. Have you eaten?"

"It doesn't matter."

Still, rather than look at her just then, he went to make her a sandwich.

"You are usually so thoughtful," said Orestes, returning, with a smile of awareness. "Believe me, Dora, I understand more than you think."

"Thank you, that looks delicious."

"How you must resent me," he went on. "How guilty you must feel for having used me."

"What do you mean, Orestes?"

"For marrying me," he said carefully as to a child, "so that you could stay in America."

She watched him, wondering how much of the truth it was needful to point out.

Orestes blushed.

"I don't know what I'm saying," he said sadly. "Both of us wanted . . ."

"Go on. Tell me, please."

"The experience. The insight. What else should one want, Dora?"

He had spoken simply. She shut her eyes, touched.

"Your generosity to me," he said, "is something I can never forget—or, it would seem, repay."

"Generosity, I don't know . . ." she echoed vaguely in order not to be silent.

*His* silence made her look. It was his turn to avoid her eyes. Ah!—"his" cottage on the property at Diblos. She smiled partly with irony—was he afraid she would ask for it back?—partly with pity. How much it must mean to him, if he could think of it now.

The mood changed. Out of habit, Orestes told Dora what he had done and whom he had seen during the week. She listened and commented, then:

"I ought to go now," she said, rising. "I shan't come to town next week. The week after, probably."

What was happening? Orestes looked at her untouched sandwich, at the cracked leatherette seats of his chairs. The phrase, 'the mother country,' lit on his mind like a flake of soot. He had been waiting for Dora to deny that she was through with him; instead, she stood at the door, an expression of perfect good nature masking her decision and conveying it in all its firmness. Her lover, he thought, the manager of the olive groves, dismissed.

In the days that followed, Orestes tried to reason that Dora was suffering from strain or fatigue or at worst from some passing mental illness; her mind had caught cold; soon she would be cured, they would again be friends. But his fantasies took off from a contrary assumption—she *was* in her right mind, she *had* dismissed him. He woke, weeping, from nightmares he hadn't had since his analysis, dreams of falling in which balconies crumbled from his grasp like birthday cake. What was this? He bent a sharp ear to his motives. The rupture evidently meant more to him than he knew.

All his life, Orestes recognized, he had been oftener at home with disciples than with friends or lovers. The last year was a remarkable exception, having brought him not only Dora but Sandy. After a certain age, however, the heart gives itself, if at all, too easily; the gift can be taken back. Orestes was nearing forty. His prime allegiance remained to his ideals or (if ever they conflicted with it) to his career.

He concluded tough-mindedly that it wasn't Dora alone he would miss, but also the security she had given him and might now withhold. He considered, marveling coldly, how much self-knowledge had brought his cottage to mind at the crucial moment, and how much delicacy had kept him from mentioning it.

He oversimplified. Years later when, back in Greece, Orestes tried to take possession of his cottage pride barely colored his motives, greed not at all. Nor did he expect, with his magic figures absent, to recapture the bliss of that time. But his tiled floor, his rock garden, his cove, the eucalyptus trees veined with leaf-gray and distant azure—a longing for these things, that is, for the sentimental truths they would still bear witness to, had been welling up in him like a madness. He was actually relieved to learn, from Dora's lawyer, that he had no claim on them whatever. It made the spirit purer in which he wrote his last letters to her. Even in America, at the time of their separation, Orestes had principally needed—since he wasn't to have her love— a view of himself as morally finer than Dora.

She had shown him her way of ending an intimacy. He wished her now to sample his. Therefore, on her next coming to town, he arranged an evening. Ceremoniously he called for her at the hotel, pinned a flower to her coat, carried her suitcase—it was Sunday. After dinner in a French restaurant, through which both talked calmly if relentlessly of joint tax returns and not bothering to divorce and a novel Dora had liked and the still unsold Bokhara, he took her to the theatre where they could hold their tongues in peace. The play was *Othello*. "It seemed more fitting to let art have the last word," said Orestes in the taxi, although by then she had seen what he was up to. In due course the beautiful words began to sound, the play to unroll like a great Venetian curtain, first abstracting their life together, then enveloping it. By the last act, Dora was asleep, muffled in gold. Her gentle snores brought it to his attention; as a detail, it seemed ironically right. In the end, screams woke her. The black actor was strangling the white actress. A violence to which all the words had been leading. She turned to Orestes, her eyes opened, inquiringly but with no single inquiry. Would it end in time for her train? came to mind along with, Would it not have helped to strangle *her*?—both frivolous questions, she knew, seeing his face lifted calm into the bluish light of the stage, the shining snail's-track of a tear drying along his nose. Soon after that it did end; she was early for her train. On the platform he remembered to give her a letter, addressed to them both, from Sandy in Colombo. Dora promised to return it, thanked Orestes for the evening, without reflecting offered him her cheek to kiss, did not take in the proud averting of his lips, and entered the coach. He stood watching her framed by her window's lighted oblong. She had made herself comfortable. Her eyes were meeting his with as much gravity as he could have wished until, the train filling up, a Negro sailor took the seat next to her, and she, hoping to make Orestes smile, raised both hands to her throat and pretended to squeeze. Through the glass she felt his sad impatience, dropped her hands, began to glide, before he could think what was happening, out of his sight.

4.viii.61
What has happened is still too strange. I can't

5.viii.61
I've seen Orson. He has come at last, and gone.

Now & then, as I've sat gazing down the lagoon
toward the Sleeping Woman, something has taken
place within me like the blowing of a fuse when too
many lights are turned on for the current to bear. The
house of these weeks has gone suddenly, magically dark,
& a joy entered me, as my ~~eyes~~ heart adjusted to
familiar shapes, & the square of moonlight brightened
on the floorboards. What I knew then reached back beyond anything I could see or remember, into a world
even my mother has forgotten, though she lives in it,
too, joyous, forever young. I have felt tremendously at
home in this knowledge. Part of me *does* belong here.
There has been no need to use words. But the lights,
each time, have had to go on again. I had been looking
for something. Soon once more the house has blazed &
the voluble search been resumed. That is ended now. I
am switching them off one by one. Have I found whatever it was? Probably not. I know chiefly that I am no
longer looking.

In fact I'm leaving. Tomorrow, Tuesday, Diblos
will lie behind me. America lies ahead, the land of op-
portunity. I have vowed to find a job before Labor Day.
I should be able to make myself very useful in a travel
agency.

I reached a standstill after copying out these last
pages, plotted & written & rewritten over 3 weeks on
separate, unlined sheets. I had hoped to escape the
tyrany of the Notebook—all my false starts, contradic-
tions, irruptions of self, bound together, irrevocably.
Books ought to consume their sources, not embalm
them.

These 'finished' pages are the best I can do. They
have their own movement, & are often believable. But
they have become fiction, which is to say, merely life-
*like*. I nearly stopped transcribing them when I came
upon that upside-down, how-many-weeks-old dream
(whose meaning is so ~~plain~~ disturbing today) & again
when that most recent entry turned up—I'd have
ripped it out but was too tired & indifferent to recopy
one side of the page already covered.

Yesterday & today I read the whole notebook
through. Actually, this last passage struck me as less
artful than the earlier ones, with all their indecisions,
pendimenti, glimpses of bare canvas, rips & ripples &
cracks which, by stressing the fabric of illusion, re-
quired a greater attention to what was being repre-
sented. (How telling my never finding a name for Dora
—only parentheses as for something private or irrelevant; and my reduction of Orson/Orestes, oftener than
not, to his initial: a zero.)

When I reread it, the finished section troubled me.
It has Dora & Orestes separating at the end of 8 months
in America, instead of the nearly four years it took them
to reach this decision. Their visit to Houston is not

described, or Sandy's to New York. I leave out dozens
of people, notably O.'s student Harriet, & their affair.
This telescoping produces a false perspective. The char-
acters, hurried through what was in fact a slow, painful
action, become often trivial, like people in a drawing-
room comedy. With Sandy absent, his viewpoint gets
transferred, and a lot of valuable space given, to *another*
3rd person, Arthur Orson, who is unnecessary to the
story, or at least figured in it differently, having refused
—but who cares! My point is that I did do my best, but,
as the Gorgon's face was mine, never succeeded in
getting a full view of it.

Throughout, I observed considerably more interest in D.'s & O.'s estrangement than in their love
for one another. Why? Did their love threaten me, or
their estrangement comfort me? It was surely no fault
of theirs if I were still on this island playing with them
in effigy, loving the effigies alone, masks behind which
lay all too frequently a mind foreign to them. Dora's
amnesia—which comes off as well as anything—is
largely my experience at the slaughterhouse (p. 17)
transformed. Would I have thought to make her feel
shame afterwards, if I hadn't felt it myself vis-à-vis
Lucine? *I* was "Dora." *I* was "Orestes." They—whoever "they" were—kept mostly beyond my reach.

"The sun & moon together in the sky."

I wanted to set down these thoughts first, before
seeing if I can write what happened on Saturday. Then
I will (figuratively) drown my book. Blind I go. Love
hasn't worked, not this year, & art isn't the answer.

I hadn't slept well. Around 11 :00 I was still half in bed, thinking of nothing, when Chryssoula knocked (she no longer enters my room, except to clean it when I'm out, there are no more bunches of basil, only a reproachful, red-eyed mask; little Theodoros brings me my tea) & deposited George eager on the threshold. Before I could catch her eye, she was gone. My first mistaken thought was that G. had come to repair his behavior of several days earlier, when, having got 200 drachmas from me on a pretext so ridiculous I believed him, he foolishly pressed his winning streak by asking outright for my pale blue slacks. "Never mind," he said—but a *friend* would not have refused him, as had I; this judgment hung in the air of our parting. I'd known all along what kind of person he was. I'd even made out through his complacency & opportunism the milky negative of those traits: loyalty to a code no middleclass foreigner would ever understand. I was sorry that things had come to a head, but relieved. Now, with my initiation into 1 local mystery (George's friendship), it seemed the exorcism of the place could begin. Those last days, I caught myself looking at Diblos as if before long I would never see it again.

"Your friends are here, get up, come quickly!" he announced with words & gestures. Friends? What friends? George groaned, cast about, pounced upon L.'s watercolor which I'd slipped into the framed hotel regulations behind the door. Those friends: the caïque! Yes, and the girl!

He sat on the bed, bouncing with excitement while I washed. I hesitated over a clean shirt; cleverly, with his hands G. shaped Lucine out of thin air—I was dressing up for her? To dampen him, I put on the pale blue slacks. We go caïque Athens, olla mazì, to-geth-er? No, my Giorgios, we do not go Athens.

Another knock—Chryssoula, dead-pan, with a scented note signed "Nicole N." They had been fleeing the heat in Hydra, could stop only an hour at Diblos, wouldn't I join them for an ouzo on the caïque? I asked her to send word back that I would be along fra poco.

Rescued!

I got rid of G., considered shaving my beard, decided to face them with it, & tumbled out of the hotel.

On the waterfront the news greeted me.

As before, Mr N. was striding up & down, and his wife emerging from the Enfant's shop. Waves of excitement. Orson had appeared! Not 15 minutes earlier, he had been rowed across from the mainland. Under the eyes of everyone but the N.'s (who were hearing about it now, at the moment of my joining them) he had sent away the boatman, left his knapsack at the café, set out on foot for the House.

A flurry of speculation & rumor. Was Byron on the island? Yes. No. He had/had not been on yesterday's boat, been seen in town earlier this morning. Was it not rather his old serving-woman who had come to buy fish? Ah, but fish was not for old serving-women. Byron himself had therefore to be in residence.

We boarded the caïque to escape all this. I asked Mr N. how Dora had responded to the letter from his office.

"*The* letter? We have written 4. Your brother has written, I should think, daily. Dora has never replied."

Had she received the letters, I wondered, or been ill?

She had received them, Mr N. was sure. Other letters sent to the same address had been answered. Byron, too, she had written—without (according to him) one line about Orson or his cottage. As for health, who knew? She was well enough to be spending the summer on Cape, what was it called? Morue in French.

Mrs N.: Cape Cod! Thoreau! Emily Dickinson!

Orson, it seemed, had pretty much grasped the situation, seen that he was making himself a nuisance, wanted to let matters drop. He had telephoned Mr N.'s office some 10 days before to say that he was leaving Athens on a walking tour & might, if he passed nearby, cross over to Diblos to pick up a few belongings he'd left there.

I told the N.'s about seeing Byron, & his hoping that O. would stop by for some books.

Mr N.: Ah well, then, that explains why he's here today.

Mrs N. (busy with ice & ouzo): The Greeks are impossible. Admit it, Akis! My gossipy shopkeeper has invented such a drama you can't imagine. If—how did you call him? If the Enfant Chic is to be believed, your brother has only to set foot on Dora's land to be driven off with a cravache by Byron.

I thought I'd misheard her. "A what?"

Mrs N.: A cravache. A whip.

Mr N.: A riding-crop. May I say that your shop-keeper, Nicole, is not one's ideal of the reliable informant?

We sipped our drinks. I was visited by the odd notion that *my* (Dora), too, would have left those letters unanswered, & that *my* Orestes would have set out, on foot, at Orson's side. There had been that much truth, after all, behind those masks.

And *my* Byron? Would he be waiting on the terrace with a whip?

A terrible guilty excitement slowly filled me. I *knew* that the Enfant had spoken the truth, & that I'd done nothing to prevent what was going to happen. A brutal, horrible action (p. 18). How could I have prevented it? In countless ways. By making friends with the E. C. By having gone to Byron's for a drink that day. By writing O., even, and trying to warn him, since I must have known in my heart that he would come to Diblos sooner or later. By not keeping this notebook! Out of myself, my inertness, as well as a few things Orson had given me (nail-parings, his secret name, a drop of his blood) it came over me that I had constructed a magic doll called Orestes, which had drawn him here. ~~I had wanted~~ Awake & asleep, I had dreamed of his punishment.

In French Mrs N. asked her husband how long a walk it was to the house. He answered.

We each calculated silently that O. would be there by now.

I looked up, needing to escape from my thoughts. Where was Lucine? It struck me that we had been sitting here on deck without her.

"Ah, Lucine," said Mrs N. "Let me see, they would be arriving in Paris tomorrow. No, today."

I felt my face change. I thought she was joking. Hadn't George seen L., said she'd come as well as the caïque? As I took it in, I had a rush of silly annoyance with *him*. And who were 'they'?

I asked, hadn't L. planned to be in Greece the whole summer?

"In Europe," said Mrs N. "She left Greece, oh, 3 weeks ago. You received the aquarelle from her? It *was* charming, I must say I hoped she had painted it for Akis and me, but she wanted you to have it. I promised to keep it for you, then sent it by mail because how did I know when we'd ever see you again?—what with your deserting us after Epidauros. I mailed it myself, the day after she left. What? Ah, your charming note. Yes, it pleased us so much. No, not alone. With a red-haired girl from Charleston or Galveston & a boy named Rob whose father is a bank president. First to Venice, then Munich, then Paris. So you've missed her!" She was bright & decisive throughout. I am still a fortune-hunter in her eyes.

She had forwarded my letter about the watercolor, & will give me an address in London good through August.

"If you were really interested you could have shown it more," said Mrs N. gaily with her eyes on my face. "Girls today don't sit in their parlors waiting for the man to make up his mind."

It was long past twelve. The heat burned through the awnings, melting our ice. The E. C. stood in his doorway. George had found several excuses to pass back & forth. By now I would surely have pointed him out to the N.'s who at any moment were going to invite him on board, offer him a drink, take him to Athens, Paris, New York. It was for our convenience, really, that he kept in sight.

His expectancy was easier than my own to understand.

A deep breath, one might have said, had been indrawn by somebody whose attention was at the same instant so caught & held by 1000 details of the scene— a hot sun-shaft, Mrs N.'s elbow corrugated by the wicker she had leaned upon, a dog on the quai, the dog's reflection in water—so held that he, the breather, simply kept forgetting to exhale. In the harbor a mullet leapt, realized its error, flopped back stunned. The N.'s themselves, who according to her note had been all eargerness to depart, sat becalmed. I cannot think what more we talked about. They did not, I know, suggest my accompanying them to Athens that afternoon. And in the end it was Orson they rescued from this island.

The scene kept brightening & darkening around me. Under his sign ("Tout pour le Sport") the Enfant's pitted moon-face shone—the face of Herodias when she says: My daughter has done well. The Sleeping Woman stirred, at intervals, on her mirror mattress.

~~Orestes~~

Orson appeared at the far end of the waterfront. Mr N. had said, "I believe . . ." The rest of us looked up.

His approach was, or seemed, slow. Something about it had caused a number of little boys to leave the beach & follow him. He couldn't have been walking too slowly; they were having to trot to keep up. From town, a handful of adolescents, as on the green radio beam of the Enfant Chic's gaze, ambled forth to meet him.

"C'est donc lui? Comme il est bronzé," said Mrs N. "Vraiment, on dirait un grec."

Mr N. (God love him): Mais, c'est un grec, idiote. Tu n'as rien compris?

~~He had been whipped He had evidently Byron had~~

We could now see the red weal on Orson's face, & stripes of red on his shirt where he had lifted his shoulder to blot it. He had on walking shorts but carried a jacket over his arm. The visit had been formal.

15 or 20 children and boys completed the procession. The Eumenides—only in this instance they were, without irony, "Kindly Ones." Their faces expressed pity & wonder, they kept pace in silence. Greeks, unlike Americans, are not thrilled by violence. Alone, the Enfant Chic called from his doorway, sarcastically, "Bon zour, Monsieur. Vous voulez quelque chose?"—and somebody did laugh.

"Ftáni, putana!" shouted an angry voice at the foot

of our gangplank. It was George. The E. C. (who had been addressed) smirked & looked debonair.

Orson was not looking our way, though close enough to have seen us on the shaded deck. Soon he was abreast of the caïque. His face was calm & exalted.

I rose from my chair. I felt the N.'s glance at me. I cannot make this sound as if it happened.

He was passing us by, keeping to the water's edge. He was clearly heading nowhere—hadn't he *become* his destination? (But 50 yards more & he would hit the path to the slaughterhouse.)

I felt my eyes sting—L. at Epidauros, surprised by the turn of events. I ran down the gangplank, caught up with him, could not speak, took his arm, & led him onto the caïque.

The dimness under the awning dazed him, other-wise he was in complete possession of himself. Even with my beard he had known me. I turned to him now, arms open. We said each other's names & embraced.

"This is what I meant in my letter," he said, step-ping back, hands still on my shoulders. "What I have wanted & never had from you."

I turned away confused.

Part of me is still glowing with pleasure at those words. Part of me is still running away from them.

He was still Orson, in any case. In a moment he too had turned & was replying to the N.'s offers of rest, re-freshment, medication in his familiar "teacher's" voice —the voice that says, 'I understand these things far bet-ter than you. They are useful but irrelevant.' Mrs N.

made him accept a glass of cognac. He sipped it & set
it down. Then Mr N. took him below to bathe his face.
Out of sight, Orson could be heard suddenly exclaim-
ing, "But pardon me, haven't we met before? Long ago,
wasn't it you who, etc."—in tones of amazed discovery,
& Mr. N.'s replies, too melodious to make out, until a
door clicked shut.

Mrs N. went to the rail & said something into the
crowd below. Several boys made a dash for the café.
Whoever got there 1st, it was George who returned
carrying O.'s knapsack. He stood at the top of the
gangplank, holding it. Mrs N. thanked him & asked
him to put it down. I forget what distracted her; when
she looked again he was still there, radiantly waiting,
so she thanked him again & he went away.

They were going to take Orson to Athens. Good.

Before she could include me in the assumption, I
approached Mrs N. & said I would have to leave them
now. I held out my hand. Like an automaton's hers
rose, hesitated, came to rest in mine.

I've promised to call on her in Athens this week.
She absolutely did not understand. But then, to do
justice to the moment, neither did I.


I went up into the hills behind the town. I climbed
& climbed, stumbling, not stopping, wanting to think.
I felt excited and confused over the way I was acting.

I saw at least how little any of it had been my doing
—for better or worse. Orson hadn't known I was on
Diblos. No one had drawn him here but himself, his

life. Betrayal & rejection are what he has always needed in his dealings with people. When Dora didn't answer his letters, what could he do but seek satisfaction at her son's hands? He hadn't deserved his whipping, rather he had all but made it happen, acting, as he had, in good faith as in bad taste, out of his own ~~blind~~ hopeless allegiance to this country of his dreams. And he had carried it off, made it seem like justice. Even I, in the notebook's blackest depths, would never have dared to construct such a denouement—coincidence, melodrama, every earmark of life's (the rival's) style. Il miglior fabbro!

~~How not to admit admire~~

How not to envy him the total experience? With courage or cunning or luck he had paid

O. had found a currency in which to pay the full price for what he believed. His view of things, his "tragic" view, would never be wholly an illusion, once having interlocked so perfectly with his suffering. I ought to have felt by contrast as I did when the Army rejected me, or like the saints who died painlessly in bed, not complaining really, only whispering the dry fact that they hadn't been found worthy of the martyr's crown.

Instead, I kept breaking into smiles—of pure aesthetic pleasure? Not entirely. I *had* been part of it. I had even paid a little price of my own: that of "missing" Lucine. Missing her, as Mrs N. had implied, by sitting here, doing whatever I was doing. Missing *in* her something I could or should have had, or have wanted at least enough to go after. What I hadn't missed by sitting on Diblos was my moment with Orson. All of it —the running after him, & his words, his hand on my shoulder; *and* the running away, while my heart was still full.

I still feel somewhat as if I had brought off a little raid on life, & escaped with my treasure intact.

I had reached the hilltop with its white chapel, door & window sliced out of unbaked meringue, a baby's confection—yet wholly itself, an innocent, arbitrary shape. I sat in the white shade, sweating, looking back. The wind blew. There below, at different points round the lagoon, were all my landmarks. I felt light & happy, & at rest.

I let the day's events play themselves once more in my head. As they did, I had a sense of other, less personal elements, beauty, joy, truth, splendor—~~things ideas~~-all whose ebbing over the years had been so gradual that I'd never registered it—flowing back now to their place at the heart of the scene, pure & compelling. In their light, Byron himself seemed not so much a spiteful neurotic as a proud

B. himself, in their light, stood forth in dark, glowing colors, velvet & gold braid, & dagger-handle flashing—a costume from the vendetta country of Crete or the Mani. Banked like a coal, his pride had burst into flame at last. He raised

In my head he raised his beautiful clenched hand. The riding-crop descended, once, twice, again, upon my

once, twice, again, inscribed its madder penstroke
upon my brother's face, at the tempo of a ~~slowly pound-~~
~~ing tempo of a giant's drugged pulse~~
of the dolphin's progress through glittering foam
at the tempo of those 3 blows whereupon the curtain of the Comédie rises to reveal, as foreseen, that
universe of classical unity whose suns blaze & seas
glitter & whose every action however brutal is nobly,
inflexibly ordered & the best of each of us steps forth in
his profound dark spotlight with poetry on his lips.

Had anyone discovered me up there, I would have
been caught in flagrante with a myth-making apparatus
every bit as vigorous as O.'s & probably a trifle more
depraved. I come back today to how little I cared for
him, how much for the idea of him.

Today I tend, in my better moments, toward
chagrin & scruple. *That* orgy must never be repeated!
—as with a moistened cloth I dab primly at my mind,
where there are telltale stains.

There is evidently *no* excuse for my having left the
caïque.

From my vantage I could watch it sail. I walked
down the hill & began to pack.


6.viii.61
My last day. Tonight I shall be in Athens. Tomorrow I'll make peace with Orson. I've got to, I want to,
before sailing home.

~~It has all been at one remove anyhow. Has the time come to tackle the Houston novel?~~

George looked in this morning. "You no go caïque? Why?"

"I go vapóri. Today."

Again: "Why?" The palm turned out & up as if to catch a grapefruit from above, the face blindly smiling, shaken from side to side—I shall miss the Greek 'Why?'

I'd left out the blue slacks he liked, & gave them to him. He printed his name & address for me. "Good my friend," he said, leaving.

I have made peace with Chryssoula, too. We have held each other, foreheads touching sadly, reflectively. My photograph is tucked face-down in her brassiere. A young Englishman has arrived with whom she can laugh tomorrow. She will find a present under my pillow—some money & a little flagon of perfume.

(While in Italy Dora & Orestes & Sandy can stop in Urbino to see the Piero *Flagellation* which O. has greatly admired in black & white.)

Orestes' disappointment was keen to discover that the punishment of the god, for all its monumental aspect in reproduction, was in fact quite small, and ~~unexpectedly~~ subtly, vividly colored.

I must be mad. I've given up this novel.

"The only solution is to be very, very intelligent." Intelligence, it is implied, will dissimulate itself, will *lose itself* in simplicity. By the same token, any extended show of Mind may be taken as the work of some final naïveté.

On deck. We have sailed past the House. The Sleeping Woman has veered & reshifted into new, non-representational masses. Diblos lies far astern. Here is the open water. A sun preparing to sink. Other islands.

# AFTERWORD

18.x.93

This little fiction, written to conceal how little of a fiction it is, like the Purloined Letter hides its strategy in plain view.

The book during its composition struck me as perilously drenched with real life. Much of it was written in the field—in the shade of the brilliant midsummer waterfront on Poros, the island where I had visited Kimon Friar and Mina Diamantopoulos on my first trip to Europe, fourteen years earlier. To be sure, Kimon and I were not half-brothers. Neither of us had a mother in Texas. "Lucine" is smuggled in from a quite different part of my life, and "Arthur Orson" is based on a fussy old man I knew in Athens, who had no connection whatever with this story. So on second thought, more invention must have come into play than I supposed at the time.

I hadn't, of course, set out to be "experimental"—heaven forbid! Ideally I would have aimed for the readability conferred by a seamless, all-knowing narrative voice. With this voice, however, I kept painting myself into a corner. Surely there were different kinds of readability, texts whose very fragmentation quickened the pulse. If the voice broke in self-revision no harm was done to the quasi-Aristotelian unity of the page. Hadn't I received letters with words scratched out? seen phrases scored through on the printed page in Buxton Forman's edition of Keats? Worth remembering was how unerringly the eye flew to precisely what the writer had thought better of: there, if anywhere, would be a truth unvarnished, which predated artifice.

Even at the time I glimpsed in my project a wistful, half-conscious critique of the Beat Generation. To Kerouac, Ginsberg, et al., revision was an all but criminal betrayal of the "spontaneity" of their vision. This view I was by temperament unable to share; true spontaneity came for me, as when Rome burned, after hours of Neronian fiddling. Thus the most successful moments in the book may well be those where the device plays with itself, when for instance a notation of the color of night ("~~dark bl~~ indigo") encapsulates the self-dramatizing "Blind I go!"

To lend weight to the device there would ideally have been some justifying narrative twist: a fact thrown into relief by its very suppression, whose discovery leaves a handful of readers wiser than the keeper of the notebook. Possibly some suspicion as to Sandy's and Orestes' "real-life" story might have been made, in more skillful hands than mine, to serve. But I was young and cavalier, and counted on the formal novelty of the book to make up for its not going very deeply into a Theme.

Sitting, then, under an awning on that blazing waterfront, at an hour when the little town nodded off, I cast about for language. When phrases took shape I welcomed them grudgingly, disdainfully, as if "we artists" were entitled to scorn our medium. But entries in a notebook also helped to pass the time, until something better came along. In another hour David Jackson would reappear to show me his afternoon's watercolor, and we could begin to think about wine and company, our reward for time so profitably spent. Those evening pleasures left no trace the next day. But their brevity and recklessness are here between the lines, if anything is.

JAMES MERRILL

# DALKEY ARCHIVE PAPERBACKS

## FICTION: AMERICAN

## FICTION: BRITISH

# DALKEY ARCHIVE PAPERBACKS

## FICTION: FRENCH

| | |
|---|---|
| CREVEL, RENÉ. *Putting My Foot in It* | 9.95 |
| ERNAUX, ANNIE. *Cleaned Out* | 9.95 |
| GRAINVILLE, PATRICK. *The Cave of Heaven* | 10.95 |
| NAVARRE, YVES. *Our Share of Time* | 9.95 |
| QUENEAU, RAYMOND. *The Last Days* | 9.95 |
| QUENEAU, RAYMOND. *Pierrot Mon Ami* | 9.95 |
| ROUBAUD, JACQUES. *The Great Fire of London* | 12.95 |
| ROUBAUD, JACQUES. *The Princess Hoppy* | 9.95 |
| SIMON, CLAUDE. *The Invitation* | 9.95 |

## FICTION: IRISH

| | |
|---|---|
| CUSACK, RALPH. *Cadenza* | 7.95 |
| MacLOCHLAINN, ALF. *Out of Focus* | 5.95 |
| O'BRIEN, FLANN. *The Dalkey Archive* | 9.95 |
| O'BRIEN, FLANN. *The Hard Life* | 9.95 |

## FICTION: LATIN AMERICAN and SPANISH

| | |
|---|---|
| CAMPOS, JULIETA. *The Fear of Losing Eurydice* | 8.95 |
| TUSQUETS, ESTHER. *Stranded* | 9.95 |
| VALENZUELA, LUISA. *He Who Searches* | 8.00 |

## POETRY

| | |
|---|---|
| ALFAU, FELIPE. *Sentimental Songs (La poesía cursi)* | 9.95 |
| ANSEN, ALAN. *Contact Highs: Selected Poems 1957-1987* | 11.95 |
| BURNS, GERALD. *Shorter Poems* | 9.95 |
| FAIRBANKS, LAUREN. *Muzzle Thyself* | 9.95 |
| GISCOMBE, C. S. *Here* | 9.95 |
| MARKSON, DAVID. *Collected Poems* | 9.95 |
| THEROUX, ALEXANDER. *The Lollipop Trollops* | 10.95 |

*(continued on next page)*

# DALKEY ARCHIVE PAPERBACKS

## NONFICTION

| | |
|---|---|
| FORD, FORD MADOX. *The March of Literature* | 16.95 |
| GAZARIAN, MARIE-LISE. *Interviews with Latin American Writers* | 14.95 |
| GAZARIAN, MARIE-LISE. *Interviews with Spanish Writers* | 14.95 |
| GREEN, GEOFFREY, ET AL. *The Vineland Papers* | 14.95 |
| MATHEWS, HARRY. *20 Lines a Day* | 8.95 |
| ROUDIEZ, LEON S. *French Fiction Revisited* | 14.95 |
| SHKLOVSKY, VIKTOR. *Theory of Prose* | 14.95 |
| WEST, PAUL. *Words for a Deaf Daughter* and *Gala* | 12.95 |
| YOUNG, MARGUERITE. *Angel in the Forest* | 13.95 |

For a complete catalog of our titles, or to order any of these books, write to Dalkey Archive Press, Illinois State University, Campus Box 4241, Normal, IL 61790-4241. One book, 10% off; two books or more, 20% off; add $3.00 postage and handling. Phone orders: (309) 438-7555.